THROUGH THE PORTAL
OF TIME

At a quarter to nine, Dr. Walker asked Tom and Cal to step onto the platform. His palms itching, his stomach faintly aching—*he was actually going through time, back nineteen hundred and eight years*—Tom tried to smile at Cal.

"Four minutes," Dr. Walker called at what seemed only an instant later.

Tom watched the multicolored lights blinking faster and faster. Would he ever see them again? See Washington? The familiar world?

"Thirty seconds. Stand by."

With the minute hand at ten before the hour, the sweep second hand hit twelve. A cool, tingling darkness enveloped Tom suddenly.

Far away, as through windy darkness, a disembodied voice seemed to call, "*Good luck—*"

When Tom opened his eyes, he was in Po

The Best in Science Fiction from SIGNET and MENTOR Books

Time
Gate

by
JOHN JAKES

A SIGNET BOOK
NEW AMERICAN LIBRARY
TIMES MIRROR

For my nephews and nieces—
Jim, Chris, Steve,
Dick, Joe, Sara,
Alice Anne, Louise, Hans Luther,
and Faris

That's ten more science fiction
readers right there

Time present and time past
Are both perhaps present in time future,
And time future contained in time past.

> —*T. S. Eliot,*
> *Four Quartets.*
> *Burnt Norton, I*

CONTENTS

1

THE RED DOOR

"HAWAII," Tom said. "Marine biology."

Dr. Calvin Linstrum put down his fork and stared across the cafeteria table. That infuriating, superior smile turned up the corners of his mouth.

"You feel you're qualified to make that decision?" he asked.

"Don't be sarcastic, Cal. I'm eighteen. It's my future."

"To waste as you wish," Cal nodded. He glanced at the clock set in the concrete wall. Ten to one. Ten minutes until Dr. Gordon White would begin his preparations for departure into the past.

Tom shoved his plate aside, no longer hungry. Every discussion with Cal ended the same way.

But he tried once more. "The university feel I'm qualified. I got a telemail from them yesterday—"

"You told me."

"But did you get the point? The university will accept me when the new term starts."

"So in two months you'll just hop off to Honolulu, fool around for four years, and *then* decide whether you're going on to grad school?"

"What's wrong with that?"

"Plenty! Education is far too important to be left to chance. We need to sit down now, map out a complete tentative program—"

"If it's not a lifetime master plan, and it doesn' bear the personal stamp of approval of Dr. Calvin Linstrum—"

"Now who's being sarcastic? I do have thirteen years on you, remember."

A short, explosive sigh from Tom. Then, "Cal, it's not that I don't appreciate all you've done since Dad died. But why does everything have to be so methodical? Planned down to the last little nit?"

"Method is the key to science, Tom."

"Well, I'm no scientific experiment!"

"True. You're my brother. I'm concerned about your future."

"Let *me* worry about my future."

"When you have the proper experience, the maturity—"

Angrily, Tom flung down his napkin. "It always comes down to that, doesn't it? You're older, you're smarter, you have all the education. Well, I get sick and tired of having you sit in judgment. As if the fact that you're carrying on Dad's work gives you the right—"

"But that's the point," Cal interrupted. "I think it does."

Heavy silence.

Cal didn't take his position out of malice, Tom knew. It was brother looking after brother, because each represented the only family the other had. Yet it was stultifying, especially when Cal's slender, bony face pulled upward into that smiling suggestion of superior wisdom.

"What makes you so certain I'm qualified for doctoral work?" Tom challenged. "You've seen my achievement scores. They're not the highest."

"Any son of Dr. Victor Linstrum can do whatever he wants in science. The name alone will open doors. That's why it's important to be careful." Cal leaned forward, his unruly reddish hair bobbing across his forehead. "You asked me how I can be certain. How can *you* be sure marine biology is it?"

"I enjoyed those field trips to the Gulf with the class—"

"High school summer excursions? Proves nothing." Cal stood up. "We'll discuss this another time."

"Let's discuss it now!"

"No, Tom. Later. When you're less resentful of the fact that I'm only trying to help."

"I'll take advice," Tom exploded. "But not orders!"

Cal picked up his tray and carried it to the load chute, where it was sucked away into the wall. "I'm glad you don't bridle so much at carrying out orders around the department," he said. "We couldn't afford an inexperienced

summer assistant who demanded that we operate the Gate
his way or not at all. Try to apply that fact to your personal affairs."

And he walked out.

Tom all but flung his tray into the chute. The stainless
steel covers clanged as air pulled the disposable dishes and
tableware down into the underground.

Why *wouldn't* Cal listen?

Sure, he was brilliant. And yes, it *was* rare for a scientist not long past thirty to be in charge of an installation
as advanced as Department 239-T. But that was because—the old bogey again!—Cal was Victor Linstrum's
elder son.

Not that Cal wasn't at home with most of the intricacies
of the time-phase effect. He was. But scientific expertise
didn't guarantee skill in dealing with other people.

And Tom was number two son. *Ipso facto*, not quite
bright. He hated the role.

The clock hand reached a minute before one. Tom hurried to the door, displayed his photo-ident to the security
cell. The door whooshed back. Tom walked down a concrete corridor, approached a soldier on duty at a massive
gray metal door. The guard wore a white helmet and a
holstered gun loaded with nerve darts. A sign on the door
read: ADMITTANCE TO AUTHORIZED PERSONNEL ONLY.

The door opened to Tom's ident. Halfway down another
short corridor, there was an alcove on the left. Under a
pin spotlight, an oil portrait of Dr. Victor Linstrum, blue-
eyed, spade-bearded, glowed softly. A small metal plaque
carried words in a fine script: NOBEL LAUREATE, 1978.

The hall ended at a large concrete antechamber with
several doors opening off each side. One led to the costume storage rooms. It was open. Tom saw Donald moving around inside.

Another door, extremely thick, was the entrance to the
department's timelock vault, which housed master records
of each archaeological mission. The vault controls were located beside the door.

A third, red-painted door led to the Gate. Tom went to
yet another door and pushed through.

Inside the brightly lighted ready room, Calvin Linstrum
was talking with a stout, florid man of middle age. Gordon
White wore his hair long, contrary to current styles. Over

the past month he had grown a gray-peppered beard. He was just hanging his shirt on a peg.

Seeing Tom, the older man held up his right hand, palm outward. *"Vale!"*

"What's that mean?" Tom wanted to know.

"You wouldn't ask that of a resident of Pompeii," White grinned. "He'd know you were wishing him good day and good luck."

"Quite the scholar, isn't he?" Cal said.

"I should be," Gordon White harrumphed. "I've practically been sleeping with those instruction machines."

"What do you need?" Tom asked.

"My toga, for one thing."

"I saw Donald in the storeroom. I think he's getting it."

"The camera and recorder, then."

"Coming up."

Tom crossed the antechamber, entered a room in which various small electronic devices were stored. From the bins he selected a matchbox-size camera that took a special hundred-exposure roll of fast film, and a tiny, egg-shaped device.

Next, by yellow light, he loaded the camera. Then he inserted a spool tape inside the tiny egg. He signed his name and ident number to his requistion and fed the punchcard into the inventory machine. The machine flashed lights and rang a bell to indicate everything cleared.

Tom started across the antechamber again. A tall, well-built young man with hair lighter than his brother's and features less sharp, less angular, he was actually taller than Cal by about three inches. Perhaps Cal resented that.

But the quarrel was forgotten as Tom's glance slid across to the closed red door.

No matter how many times he saw a temporal archaeologist depart, he never quite grew accustomed to the idea. In the stillness of the underground, with only the air conditioners whispering, the old feeling of wonder returned.

It seemed remarkable—awful, in the original sense of that word—that in less than two hours, Dr. Gordon White would walk through the red door to the Gate, then emerge on a plain outside Roman Pompeii, four days before the city was destroyed by the eruption of Mount Vesuvius—

Seventy-nine years after the birth of Christ.

Of all the secret departments of the United States Government, none was more secret than the one known by the innocuous designation Department 239-T.

Its modest operating appropriation, passed routinely by Congress every year, was concealed in the budget of the Department of Defense. Department 239-T came under the jurisdiction of Defense almost by default. Government planners believed there might be potential military application for the secret contained in 239-T's underground bunker. But no planner had yet found a way to apply the secret on a risk-free basis.

The White House exercised close personal control over 239-T's operations, to make sure no one tried to employ the Gate for short-sighted gains, because no one really knew what the consequences might be.

Even Victor Linstrum, the man who had put together the mathematical-physical base for the Gate in 1974, had not been able to calculate all possible consequences, though he guessed at many. Concerned about his discovery's ultimate use, he approached the Government with caution. Fortunately, he found an understanding administration. The Government funded construction of the bunker as one of many basic research expenditures. Eventual payoff, if any, was unknown. The then-President was sensitive to potential dangers when Dr. Linstrum explained them. Each of the two succeeding chief executives had been equally perceptive.

Dr. Calvin Linstrum had been in charge of the facility since the death of the elder Linstrum five years earlier, in 1982. Department 239-T functioned solely as a lab for an entirely new kind of research—temporal archaeology. For, by means of the Gate, travel forward and backward in time was now possible.

So far, there had been only limited, and cautious, use of the Gate. No one knew, for example, what would happen if a twentieth-century man appeared in Washington at the end of the War Between the States and prevented the murder of President Lincoln. All sorts of tampering with historical events was theoretically possible. But the hazards were far too great to be tolerated.

Indeed, at the insistence of the President, time-tampering experiments were not even contemplated.

Department scholars traveled back in time to selected historical sites. They were costumed in the style of the period and equipped with a basic knowledge of the language and customs, plus appropriate coinage. Thus they were able to blend into the culture reasonably well.

Temporal researchers were permitted to do only three things: observe; take photographs; and make sound recordings, using unobtrusive, miniaturized gear. Victor Linstrum had insisted on no disturbance of the milieu into which the time traveler ventured.

For this reason, travel forward in time had been tried only in a limited way. A few short trips, no more than twenty-four hours into the future, had been undertaken to prove the idea's feasibility. Even then, travelers weren't permitted to leave the department—no scrutiny of the next day's newspaper was allowed, for example. If Cal had his way, trips to the distant future would never be routine. It was logically impossible for anyone to prepare to blend in, physically or linguistically, with unknown societies of the future.

The temptation was great to employ the Gate for a look at the years immediately ahead. But so far, the President had successfully restrained those members of the military who argued most vocally in favor of it.

Because of the explosive potential of the Gate, the Government had long ago decided that its existence should not be revealed to the public. There would be too many pressures. Until you found the true potential of a weapon that might do inestimable damage, you did not play with the weapon, whether expediency prompted experimentation or not.

As Tom continued across the antechamber, the red door slid aside. A dark-haired man stuck his head out.

"Hello, Dr. Stein."

"Save me a trip, will you, Tom? Dr. Walker and I have finished the checkout. We'll be ready by three."

"I'll tell Cal," Tom nodded, moving on.

The door from the outer corridor opened. Tom saw a lift truck piled with large sealed cartons. The cartons bore the name and address of a New York theatrical costume house. The owners, Tom thought, must wonder why the Federal Government ordered eighteenth-century perukes and American Indian breeches.

The guard pointed to the storage rooms. The lift truck driver—another uniformed soldier—shifted gears and rolled his vehicle ahead.

What was keeping Donald? Tom saw no sign of anyone moving back in the bays where the costumes were racked.

In the ready room, Cal and Gordon White were still discussing the mission. Tom reported the successful checkout of the Gate equipment. A tall, gangly young man entered, carrying a plain gray toga, sandals, and several arm rings.

"You're late," Cal said.

"Sorry," Donald Koop said, though he didn't sound it. "I took five minutes to read the news. Archy's pushing disarmament again. When will he learn that the only way to deal with the Comchins is to punch them, not pat them? He'll have us surrendering yet."

Cal held out his hand. "The costume, Donald. We can do without your political commentary."

Gordon White said, "Lord knows I'm no superpatriot, but it does run against my grain to hear you call President Archibald 'Archy.' "

"His friends call him that," Donald answered. "I've met him, you know."

"Yes," Cal said, "We know."

Behind Cal's back, Donald grinned at Tom, as if to say that the attitudes of older people were beyond comprehension.

Donald Koop was even taller than Tom, and slender to the point of emaciation. He had a high forehead, accentuated by a hairless skull. The college fashion these days was a shaved pate. Donald wore round spectacles tinted blue—the most popular current shade. His white smock looked as though it hadn't been laundered in weeks.

Two years older than Tom, and an Ivy League poli sci major during the winter, Donald Koop had won his position as a summer assistant in the department through the efforts of his uncle, Senator Koop. Cal didn't care for Donald, perhaps because he had been politely forced to add the young man to his staff.

Dr. White donned a pair of coarse woolen underdrawers, then pulled the toga over his head. He slipped on the arm rings and the sandals. A wide elastic belt went around his waist beneath the toga. Special pockets held the matchbox camera and the little egg-shaped recorder.

"You forgot the cloak," White said.

Expressionless, Donald left. He returned with a long piece of wine-red wool, which White draped over his shoulders and looped across his left arm.

"Am I the perfect picture of a Roman citizen or am I not?"

"You will be when you take off your class ring," Cal said.

"Oops." White removed the gold signet.

Donald, meantime, had wandered over to speak to Tom in a low voice. "Did you read about Archy's latest proposals?"

"Haven't had time."

"I tell you, somebody has to do something about that man. Three years in office, and he's forcing the country into a totally defenseless posture. He just made public the disarmament plan he started drawing up last March. He wants to scrap all missiles—"

"That isn't exactly a new idea. It goes back to Eisenhower."

"But this time the Comchins are listening!"

"I happen to like the President's policies," Tom countered. "I guess there are some things friends don't have to agree on."

"I'll bring you around one of these days," Donald said.

Often Tom wondered whether his friend actually believed some of the outrageous ideas he espoused. He always sounded as though he did.

Dr. Walker appeared at the door. "Phone, Cal. The White House."

Cal frowned. "Transfer it in here."

"Can't. They want you to take it on the scrambler in your office."

Cal left. When he returned, he looked puzzled and unhappy. "Ira Hand will be paying us a special visit at three o'clock."

White's brow hooked up. "The Vice-President?"

Cal nodded. "His secretary sounded upset."

Donald and Tom exchanged glances. Ira Hand, liaison between President Benjamin Archibald and all the various scientific programs and departments of the Government, personally oversaw operation of the Gate facility, visiting it regularly. But the visits were always announced at least one day in advance.

White stepped to a mirror and jutted out his chin, applying a comb to his beard. "I'm flattered to have the eminently distinguished Vice-President come down expressly to witness my—"

"Cut the clowning, Gordon," Cal scowled. "Hand isn't coming here for your benefit. The Vice-President's disturbed by rumors that his office has picked up."

"Rumors?" Tom said. "What kind?"

"That there may be a security leak in this department."

2

WHO IS SIDNEY SIX?

"SECURITY LEAK?" Gordon White repeated, stunned. "With things run as tightly as they are down here? Sometimes I get the feeling I can't even tell myself what I'm doing."

The forced lightness was lost on Cal. He paced back and forth. "I don't see how it could happen either. We take every conceivable precaution—"

"Including a week of tests and interrogation just to get a part-time job," Donald said.

"But if even the possibility of a leak exists," Cal added, "we need to know."

Strain was apparent on his face. Tom lost all feeling of animosity. At a time like this, the bond between brothers was strong. Whatever Cal's faults, he took his job of carrying on Victor Linstrum's work with utter seriousness and dedication.

"Hand's secretary said the Vice-President would try to arrive a little before three," Cal told them. "Let's review the Pompeii plan once more, Gordon. Then I want to double-check the Gate, Tom—Donald—that's all for now."

"We can watch Dr. White leave, I hope," Tom said.

Cal nodded in a vague way as he left, with White right behind.

Donald rubbed his shaved head. "Personally, I'll take Hand over Archy any day. Hand believes in a strong defense posture."

10

Tom's mind was elsewhere. "Are we still going to the gem races tonight?"

"Right. Six thirty. My place. How about helping me put those new costumes away?"

"Sure."

In the storage rooms, overhead lights cast pools of yellow in the aisles between the racks and shelves. The pile of costumer's cartons had now grown to three times its original size. Delivery had been completed while they were in the ready room, Tom guessed.

Despite the lights, the vast storage area had a ghostly quality, perhaps because the hanging costumes made Tom feel that he was in the presence of disembodied people from the past: men of colonial times, dandies of Restoration England, lords of ancient Manchu China—

"We'll never get all these put away this afternoon," Donald complained. Using a knife, he slit the tape on the first box and checked the contents against an inventory list. He marked the list with a blue marking pen. Then he scribbled blue letters and a number on the carton's side.

"Mongol. Late twelfth century." Donald tapped the pen against the code scrawled on the box. "There's the shelf position."

Tom picked up the carton. He walked by a cluttered table with a newspaper lying on top. The headline caught his eye:

PRESIDENT VACATIONS AT CAMP LOOKOUT.
Prepares Draft of Latest Disarm Plan.

A paragraph of the story had been encircled. Something about the paper struck Tom as odd, some detail that registered in his mind unconsciously. As he walked down a gloomy aisle, he tried to figure out what it was. He couldn't. He'd have to look at the paper again.

While Donald put the next carton away, Tom returned to the table. The paragraph that had been encircled—with a blue marking pen—related to the probable time of President Archibald's departure from Camp Lookout, his personal retreat in the Adirondack Mountains. The story had a strange familiarity, though Tom couldn't say why. Perhaps it was because the President was always working on some version of a disarmament proposal.

Frowning, Tom scanned the page a second time. He still couldn't understand.

Suddenly, annoying because it was so obvious, he saw it.

The date of the newspaper was March 12. A weekend five months ago. No wonder the story sounded familiar.

Tom remembered the widely publicized mountain sojourn from which Archibald had returned with a first draft of a new set of recommendations for the United Nations. The President had been refining them these past months and was due to present the proposals to the world forum in person in two weeks.

Hearing Donald return, Tom picked up the paper. "For somebody who dislikes the President, Donald, you're keeping a pretty accurate history on him."

Behind the blue lenses, Donald Koop's eyes were unreadable. "Let me have that."

"Sure, but I'm curious about why—"

"I'm writing a report." Donald grabbed the paper, folded it, stuffed it into his back pocket.

"On Archibald? In the summer? On both counts, old buddy, I know you better than—"

"Look, we've got work to do."

"Hey, don't get sore."

"I'm not. I just want to get this stuff put away, so your brainy brother doesn't give me another of his lectures about efficiency."

With slashing motions, Donald used the knife to attack the tape on the next carton. Tom had seldom seen his friend so angry.

They worked in near-silence until a gong sounded. Most of the first batch of costumes had been stored, but the newest cartons hadn't been touched.

Dr. Walker, a tall man, stuck his shaved head in the door, announcing, "The Vice-President and his party have arrived."

"But it's only two thirty," Tom said.

Dr. Walker shrugged. "They want to see everyone in Cal's office, pronto."

Calvin Linstrum's personal office was a cement-block room off the central chamber. Harshly lighted and crowded with files, piles of reports, and government forms, the office barely held all those assembled: Cal, Gordon White, Doctors Stein and Walker, two other department technicians, two secretaries, Tom, Donald, and Vice-President Ira Hand and his party.

The Vice-President was a short, stocky man. He had a heavy jaw and a style of choppy gesturing that made him an effective platform speaker. He had brought a thin young man with a briefcase, who was one of his aides, plus a nondescript man in a gray suit, a stranger.

Vice-President Hand introduced the stranger promptly. "This is Mr. Sloat, my personal contact in the Justice Department. I want him to give you the same story he gave me yesterday."

Cal said, "Fire away."

Said Sloat: "Our sources have come up with a distressing rumor that may have a basis in fact. Are you all familiar with the name Sidney Six?"

Cal balanced a pencil between his fingertips. "The syndicated journalist?"

"The syndicated muckraker would be more like it," Dr. Walker said. "Mister Sensationalism. Specialist in the exposé. Long on headlines, short on facts."

Sloat smiled tightly. "You have the picture. It's possible that Sidney Six has gotten wind of the existence of this department."

"Good Lord!" White exclaimed. "Our affairs could be hanging on the public clothesline in no time."

Ira Hand nodded. "That's why we want each of you full-time employees to double your guard. Sorry, Sloat, go on."

"How Sidney Six could have gotten on the trail of this story, no one knows. How far he's developed his leads—if at all—is another unknown. The real problem lies with Six himself. You see, no one knows what the man looks like."

The stocky Dr. Stein rubbed an index finger across his old-fashioned beard. "You know, you're right. I've read his material. Dreadful stuff. But I've never seen his picture. That's unusual for a reporter with such a following."

"It's deliberate," Sloat confirmed. "Six uses assumed identities—falsified papers—we can't imagine what all—to gain entrance to wherever he wants to go. The fact that nobody knows what he looks like helps him get away with it. Do you remember those holograms of the Darien sub pens that were published a year ago?"

Nods.

"Sidney Six got them. He got into that highly guarded

installation and out again before anybody realized he was there. To this day, my department has no clear idea of whom he impersonated, or how he carried it off. That's an embarrassing admission. I make it simply to emphasize the seriousness of the problem if Sidney Six indeed decides that his next target is this department."

Cal looked slowly from face to face, trying to smile. "Okay, Sidney, where are you?"

There was uneasy laughter. On stumpy legs, Vice-President Hand walked to the center of the group. "Whatever new security measures are necessary, Dr. Linstrum, take them. I say again, ladies and gentlemen—until the Government ultimately hammers out an official time-travel policy, we cannot afford a clamor in the press. In the Gate we have a very, very tricky capability. I certainly do not understand all its ramifications—"

"No one does," Cal said. "We're like cavemen with one plug, one lamp,—and no knowledge of how far we can, or should, go in taking advantage of electricity."

"If Sidney Six penetrates this department," Ira Hand went on, "he would have absolutely no scruples about publishing the story worldwide. And we'd have investigating committees, blue-ribbon panels, editorial opinions—indeed, the President might well be forced to shut the department down. Our best course remains what it has been since 239-T was organized by your late father. Careful, considered historical research, taking care to disturb no milieu into which your people venture. We will make this facility public knowledge when we have gathered enough data to prove beyond doubt that the Gate can safely be used for unlimited travel to the past. That and only that will forestall public panic."

Cal stood up. "Thank you for spelling out the situation, sir. We'll be on watch. Though against what—or whom—I wish we knew. We can start by having a new crew of military guards assigned to the outer corridors. Guards who've been freshly screened."

"You don't suspect any of the boys on duty now?" White asked.

"No, Gordon. But evidently we can't be too careful."

Sloat said, "I'll arrange for the computers to select the men. We'll have them tested, investigated, and on duty the day after tomorrow. I guarantee Sidney Six won't be one of them." He paused. "If that's all—I gather there's a departure coming up?"

"Mr. Sloat would like to watch," Ira Hand said. "I've okayed it."

"Fine," Cal said, walking toward the door. "This way."

"To where?" Sloat wanted to know.

"To the eve of the destruction of the city of Pompeii."

Moments later, the red door slid closed behind them.

A dark tunnel showed golden light at the end. The footsteps of the party rang and echoed. Tom's pulses picked up, as they always did when he saw the Gate.

To step into another epoch, walk the strange streets, listen to an ancient language—one day, he'd have that thrill.

The Gate proper was a stainless steel platform one foot above the floor of the circular room at the end of the tunnel. The room was thirty feet in diameter, its wall completely filled with dials and switches. Around a cluster of gold floodlights in the ceiling, computer display boards flashed tiny lights in sequence.

Dr. Stein picked up a clipboard with a sheaf of closely written notes. He began checking readings on the various dials and displays.

"Forgive me," Sloat said, "but is this all there is to it?"

"This is only the operating center," Cal replied, as Dr. White stepped onto the stainless steel platform. His face, hands, and legs were several shades darker than they had been earlier. "Thirty times this amount of gear is buried beneath us."

"A computer does most of the work of relating the two coordinates," Walker said.

"Temporal and spatial," Cal explained. "Time and space. We must locate the researcher in both. And carefully. The computer handles the billions and billions of calculations necessary to make sure Gordon doesn't arrive on the wrong day—or land in the Tyrrhenian Sea. I doubt that you have any idea of the complexities involved, Mr. Sloat. Consider all the various calendars that have been in existence since A.D. 79, each slightly different from the next. They must all be taken into account."

"I'm sure the technicalities are beyond me," Sloat nodded. "My chief question is, How safe is it?"

"I've been to ancient Babylon," White said.

"I watched the battle of Waterloo last week," added Stein.

"And they haven't lost one of us yet," Walker concluded.

"You might describe some of your precautions, Dr. Linstrum," Ira Hand suggested. Tom noticed Donald Koop watching the Vice-President closely, an expression of almost mystic adoration on his face.

"Right," Cal said. "A week prior to a field trip, we begin programming the spatial and temporal coordinates. It can be done much faster, of course. But we like to be careful. We recheck the coordinates upward of two dozen times. Right now, Gordon's coordinates are locked in. The hard work's done. It's a simple matter to send him off."

"Equally simple to bring him back?" Sloat asked.

"We try to make it so. You know about our rules?"

"Only observation via camera and sound recorder? Yes, the Vice-President mentioned those."

"Gordon carries the camera and the recorder in a special belt under his toga. Plus the Gate control unit."

Dr. White fished out a small, shiny box about twice as large as the matchbox-size camera.

"That's our most important failsafe," Cal explained. "Should the researcher encounter an emergency, pressure on the side of that box returns him here instantly. It's preferable that he return from the spot where he landed in the other time. Any other location presents risks, but it's not impossible. Also, only one researcher is allowed to use the Gate at any given time. And he, in effect, controls the entire operation from the moment he vanishes from this room."

Sloat walked around the platform. "How so?"

"Because of certain relays built into the equipment, no one else at this end can go anywhere in the past except where the original researcher has gone. When our controls are properly set, the time-phase waves remain focused—locked—on the first site."

Sloat digested this slowly. "You mean that once Dr. White departs, if I decide I want to see the battle of Iwo Jima—programming all these gadgets accordingly—I'll still wind up in Pompeii?"

"Exactly. We must keep the passage between *then* and *now* open because we have no way of foreseeing what sort of trouble the research man might run into. Despite all his linguistic study, for example, Gordon could still be spotted as a stranger in Pompeii. He's applied that deep-deep-stain makeup, but he still doesn't look precisely Latin. Well—anything else?"

Sloat shook his head. "Amazing."

"Staggering might be a better word," said Ira Hand. "Do you wonder that mere human beings have trouble deciding how the Government should utilize this phenomenon?"

In the ensuing silence, Tom thought of the wonders Gordon White would soon encounter. Strange new sights, smells, sounds that ordinary archaeologists could only speculate about from the evidence of Pompeii's wall paintings and bits of shattered clay.

Dr. Stein started snapping down switches. "Two minutes," Dr. Walker announced.

"When will he be back, Dr. Linstrum?" Sloat inquired.

"In about three days, our real time. Just before Mount Vesuvius erupts. Are you familiar with the Pompeii story?"

"Vaguely."

"She was one of the finest cities of the Empire. Perched on the west coast of Latium—Italy—at the foot of the volcano. Vesuvio, as they called it. Legends say the god Heracles founded the city. A great many notable people had lavish seacoast villas in and around the city. Cicero, for one. Some scholars have called Pompeii the Monte Carlo of old Rome. In A.D. 63, an earthquake destroyed many of the public buildings. The residents were just finishing major restorations in 79 when the real destruction hit."

"The eruption of the volcano," Sloat nodded.

"Thousands died. The city was buried under tons of ashes and cinders. Archaeologists didn't start digging up the remains until the eighteenth century, when—"

"One minute," Dr. Walker called.

A sheen of sweat had built up on White's face, glistening in his salt-and-pepper beard. The top of his head was bathed gold by beams from the ceiling. The sequencing of the lights grew more rapid.

Suddenly Sloat said, "But going back there with a knowledge of the language and knowing what was—is about to happen—couldn't he warn them?"

"And save countless lives," Cal nodded. "Theoretically. The danger is, we have no way of knowing how that would affect the course of history afterward."

Ira Hand said, "And there is no person in this room—in this nation—or anywhere, so far as I know—who is prepared to accept the responsibility for a decision of that magnitude. That is why we cannot allow someone like Sidney Six—"

Cal gestured in warning.

The sequencing lights flashed faster across the blue lenses hiding Donald Koop's eyes. Dr. White started to raise his hand in a farewell gesture—

The stainless steel platform was empty.

Reflections rippled across its polished surface. Cal turned to his visitors. "Now comes the hard part, gentlemen. All we can do is wait."

3

TRACK DUAL

"LADIES AND GENTLEMEN," boomed an amplified voice, "five minutes until the main event of the evening. Twenty laps for a two-thousand-dollar purse—"

"I bet a friend that Geyser Hankins will take it," Donald said, following Tom down the steep aisle to their seats.

"He's a rough driver," Tom said, balancing the cup of iced vitabeverage with one hand while he wiped mustard off his lip with the other. "He shaves the rules pretty closely."

Donald grinned. "That's typical of you, Thomas. You let a lot of nice little scruples stand in the way of a goal. Geyser Hankins wants to win. He does what it takes to be first around that track."

Donald bit into a chocolate-covered cereal bar. "Sometimes I think there's nothing you want badly enough," he added. "When a normal person wants something, he goes after it. Or has Calvin browbeaten that out of you?"

Tom found himself irritated. "I think I'm as normal as the next guy. But I won't go after what I want regardless of the price. Doing that nullifies the worth of whatever you're after."

"A pretty little philosophy. Lucky for us, the movers of this world think otherwise. Hey! Here they come!"

A gate opened beside the banked oval track below. The track, erected around the rim of the Sportsdrome for tonight's races, consisted of interlocking slabs of a very light but firm blown foam. The gems needed only that

19

kind of resistant surface for their air currents to push against.

The Sportsdrome was Washington's newest public building, a gleaming, air-conditioned enclosed hemisphere. The tiers of seats were jammed with fans, who roared as the first of the small ground-effect machines glided onto the track.

The lime-green racer carried a large yellow numeral 7, plus a decal that identified the helmeted driver, Typhoon McGee. McGee, a black, held up his glove in a fist. His partisans yelled and applauded.

The second gem nosed onto the track. Its supporters let the driver hear their enthusiasm. All the gem jockeys seemed to affect nicknames associated with windstorms or air currents, which was natural, considering that the light, swift racers skimmed along on jets of air blowing from their underbellies. They never touched the special roadbed.

Donald said, "I'm having some friends in afterward, Thomas. Want to come over?"

This was a surprise to Tom. Donald explained that he had arranged the party at the last minute. "So the guy I made the bet with will be there. To pay off."

Tom replied, "Sure. I haven't seen the new place yet. You like it?"

"Living by yourself takes getting used to. I depended on Mom pretty heavily. But I eat over at the Senator's a lot, so that helps." Donald took off his glasses and pinched the bridge of his nose. For an instant his veneer of tough pragmatism dropped away. "I couldn't stand our old place after Mom died. Too many ghosts."

Another gem racer joined the four already at the starting line. The applause and shouting grew louder with each new arrival—the favorites usually made their appearance toward the last. The program said Hankins would be the final driver. He had won the pole position in the draw.

Tom wondered whether the friends Donald referred to shared his political views. If so, Tom was prepared to dislike them. In the last decade, student activisim had swung from the ultraleft to the extreme right. And Donald parroted all the militant slogans.

Donald had first come to work in the department the preceding summer. But it seemed to Tom that his friend's views had hardened since then, or at least he had become more vocal.

Perhaps it was partly due to the emotional shock of his mother's tragic death on an operating table. At any rate, Donald had an intense, even haggard look lately. But he was bright and, in most ways, a pleasant companion.

"Here comes the tiger!" Donald shouted, on his feet.

A sleek black racer painted with jets of red-tinged steam nosed through the gate. Just under the cowl, Geyser Hankins' name appeared in flame-colored letters. Some older fans nearby glared at Donald, then booed. Throughout the Sportsdrome, a chorus of disapproval mingled with scattered applause.

The racers began final maneuvering for starting positions. Giant floodlamps in the 'drome's ceiling poured light onto the lacquered cowls. Geyser Hankins' black helmet flashed with hard highlights.

"You don't seem very interested tonight, Thomas."

"I was thinking about Dr. White."

"Come on, Geyser!" Donald yelled suddenly. "Knock that bum if he won't move!"

Hankins was doing just that, nudging the driver on his right to make more room at the line. The bumped driver looked angry. Hankins ignored him.

The starter began his climb to the metal tower overlooking the track's inner edge.

As the stands quieted, awaiting the start, Donald said, "I'm beginning to think trips like White's are a farce anyway. I could find less trivial ways to use the Gate."

"Such as?"

"Here you have one of the most powerful—or potentially powerful—tools for change in the history of the world. What does Archy do with it? Nothing!"

"Keep your voice down! You know we're not supposed to mention—"

"Ah, these people wouldn't believe it if we diagrammed it. They're lumps, Thomas, just like most men. Squeezed out of the mold that society, and the Government, creates for them. The Government's gotten too big. Too powerful. An individual can't make a mark. He's too far removed from the decision points. That's why I get so infuriated about the Gate. Think of how it could be used, selectively, to change things."

"You mean tinker with the past?"

"Sure! Look. What if, right now, someone traveled back

to Germany circa 1933 and removed Adolf Hitler? No
World War II! Millions of human lives saved!"

"My father wrote about that sort of theory," Tom said.
"It supposes that time—the past—is like a road that can
be made to fork. Here we are, down at the end of a line
of history that began—okay, let's say in 1933. But if there
hadn't been a Hitler, A Second World War, would we be
here? Would the Sportsdrome be here? Who knows? And
back in the '40s, would this country have worked so hard
to develop the atom bomb, and all the atomic generating
plants that have come in its wake? Would we have cap-
tured the German scientists who helped us to land
Armstrong on the moon? Would we have learned how to
mass-produce penicillin? How much or how little would
everything change because of your one suggested alter-
ation? No one knows. And my father wasn't willing to experiment to find out. Cal isn't either. Besides, there isn't
just one place where the road can fork. There are millions,
when you count minor historical events. It would be foolish to try to manipulate the present via the past."

Donald snorted.

"You don't buy that?"

"No. It's a crime for that Gate to sit there, a real means
of getting things accomplished—"

"But who would decide on what to change, Donald?
You?"

"I have a few ideas."

"Name one."

"I'd go back and make sure Archy didn't get elected in
'84. With the Comchins building up strength in Asia, we
don't need his brand of mealymouthed pacifism."

Disturbed by his friend's vehemence, Tom countered,
"So you'd use the Gate to ensure his defeat three years
ago?"

"I'd use the Gate to get him out of office. Period. I—"

A pistol crack whipped their attention to the track. The
gem racers shot forward in a glittering row, riding less
than a foot off the hard-surfaced track, their airblowers
blasting and whistling. In a matter of one lap, Typhoon
McGee had taken the lead, skimming over into the pole
position an eighth of a lap ahead of Geyser Hankins.

"Catch him, Geyser!" Donald shouted, on his feet, waving his fists. "Knock him off!"

The race quickly became a duel between McGee and

Hankins, obviously driving the two fastest machines. Donald screamed Hankins' name until his voice began to grow hoarse.

During the sixteenth lap, while the other ground-effect machines fought for secondary positions, Hankins at last found the power to edge up on the leading driver. He swung his racer out to the right of McGee as they sped into one of the high-banked curves.

"Knock him out, Geyser!" Donald yelled. *"Kill him!"*

Hankins slotted over to the left, trying for position ahead of McGee. The tail of his racer slammed McGee's right front. McGee wobbled to the left. His left-hand air jets ran off the track rim and suddenly had nothing to push against. McGee fought for control as Hankins zipped into first place in the pole lane.

Hanging half on, half off the edge of the track, McGee's machine slowly tilted. Finally he lost control altogether. The nose of his racer veered sharply to the left.

McGee's machine dropped eight feet to the brilliant green artificial turf and landed belly down with a heavy thud. Smoke began to pour from the power compartment.

All over the Sportsdrome, fans were on their feet, most of them booing Hankins' tactics. Cheeks glistening with sweat, Donald applauded. His ugly expression made Tom wonder again about him.

Hankins now had a full lap's head over the nearest contender.

Donald's blue lenses loomed as he turned to laugh. "See what I mean? When Hankins wants something, he gets it."

"At any price—right?"

"That's the way the movers get things done."

"Then the movers and I don't see eye to—"

"Good for you, killer, you did it!" Donald cried, as Hankins took the checkered flag.

A rescue crew was foaming down McGee's machine to prevent fire. Other men used crowbars to pry open the driver's bubble. Moments later, McGee climbed out. Limping, he waved to the crowd. He received a sympathetic round of cheers—and a raspberry from Donald. Tom decided that he was not in a mood for a party with Donald and his radical friends.

But, watching Donald's ferocious face as he applauded Geyser Hankins pulling in to accept the purse and trophy, Tom changed his mind.

It might be smart to meet Donald's crowd. It might give him a valuable insight into the extent of Donald's rather wild convictions.

"Good for you, killer!" Donald kept shouting above the din. *"Good for you!"*

After the races, the two young men used Tom's small exhaust-free electric for the drive to Donald's flat. Tom had bought the car secondhand, with money from his earnings in the department. In about half an hour, the car brought them to an area where large apartments had been put up as part of urban redevelopment.

The night air was heavy with the threat of rain. They took the lift up to Donald's rented efficiency on the next-to-top floor, where about a dozen students Donald's own age had already gathered.

Uniformly, the young men displayed shaved heads and glasses with lenses of various colors. Tom noticed only three girls, one quite fat. They all had the drab, faintly pop-eyed look that Tom characterized—with a suitable lack of interest—as "intense."

A military march blared from the four-corner sound system. The air smelled sweet. About half the guests were smoking a legal variant of marijuana. Tom never used the stuff, for the same reason that many people, years ago, had avoided cigarettes, now long banned from public sale—he liked to feel in perfect shape, all his faculties sharp, all the time.

"Throw your jac in the bedroom and grab a high in the kitchen," Donald said. Then he shouted into the blue haze pierced by a couple of pin spotlights, "You owe me, Karlberg. Geyser took the race."

In the hall leading past the tiny bedroom, a circular dart board hung on the wall. A news photo of President Archibald had been pasted to the board. Three darts stuck from the hole-pocked photo, one in the chief executive's mouth, one in each of his eyes. Tom shivered.

Carrying a pop-open can of high, one of the girls blocked Tom's path. "Are you here about the demo?"

"Demo? No, I'm a friend of Donald's—"

The girl's face froze. "Forget I asked." She hurried on.

Tom turned into the bedroom. It was sparsely furnished—a bed, a bureau, two chairs. The focus of attention was a huge American flag tacked to the wall above the bed. A rotating multicolored plastic disc, mounted in front of a ceiling spot, cast changing patterns of red, white, and blue over the national emblem.

Tom threw his jac on the bed and headed for the kitchen. There, two bald students were discussing the "demo" the girl had mentioned. The conversation stopped a moment after Tom walked in.

He took a can of a popular brand of high from the fridge, popped the ring, let the sweet, mildly carbonated beverage relieve his thirst. He heard a faraway rumble of thunder.

In about sixty seconds, he began to experience a pleasurable sense of relaxation. High was the nickname for a generic chemical that had been developed in a major research lab a few years earlier. Invented as a substitute for hard liquor, it induced a mile euphoria without impairing judgment or motor performance, no matter how much was consumed. It left no traceable aftereffects. A sort of pop containing chemical mood lifters, it was consumed in vast quantities by young and old—much to the relief of police forces, which no longer had to contend with a high percentage of drunk drivers.

One of the students said to the other, "We plan to leave on a Tuesday. The bus is already chartered. We should be in Manhattan by—"

A nudge from the other student, obviously meant as a reminder of Tom's presence, silenced the first speaker. Both stared.

"Haven't seen you around here before," one said to Tom.

"Right. Friend of Donald's. But I'm interested in the demo. When is it?"

More scrutiny. Thunder rumbled. The military march blared.

At last one of the students shrugged and said, "Archy's presenting his latest disarmament offers to the United Nations in a couple of weeks. He's in for a big surprise when he stands up to speak in the Assembly."

"What kind of surprise?"

"First, there'll be a massive sidewalk demo, marching, singing, in front of the building when he arrives."

"But that's not all," said the other student. "Archy is going to learn that power belongs to the people in this coun-

try, or Archy isn't going to be around very long. We have
plans that will shake—"

A wagging motion of the other student's head prompted
caution again. The second student said, "You'd better talk
to Donald."

"Sounds interesting," Tom said. "I will."

In truth, it sounded appalling. The more he saw of Donald's friends, the less he liked them.

Sipping from his can of high, he returned to the living
room. His friend was surrounded by five others, all of
them shouting above the music. Tom dropped into a corner, propped himself against the wall, drank again. The
room had a dim, dreamy quality. Clouds of sweetish blue
smoke turned slowly through the slanting light beams.

There's something dangerous here, he thought.

After half an hour of being ignored, Tom got up. Donald was still arguing. Tom slipped to the edge of the
crowd.

"Have to move out, Donald. It's late."

Weaving slightly, Donald broke from the group. "Not
exactly your kind of rally, eh, Thomas? These people are
pretty involved—"

"That is *not* the best corner for forming up the demo,"
a girl shrilled. "I'll prove it! Donald, where's that map we
marked?"

"Top drawer, in the bedroom." To Tom, "So we can't
interest you in a little political activisim tonight?"

"Nor any night, thanks anyway." With a forced smile,
he told Donald he would see him tomorrow. Donald
waved and went back to his wrangling friends.

Tom passed the map fetcher just leaving the bedroom.
He found his jac, started to put it on. As he did so, his
eyes drifted toward the bureau. The top drawer was half
open. Sticking out from under a Harvard sweatshirt was
an object whose shape Tom recognized instantly.

He glanced at the door. No one was coming.

He moved to the bureau in two quick steps, and lifted
the sweatshirt. Among tangled T-shirts lay a black needle-
muzzle laser pistol.

The i.d. plate below the light-amp chamber had been
filed bare. Bought illegally, then. Only contraband
weapons had the federal registration serial removed.

What earthly use did Donald Koop have for a laser pistol?

Suddenly Tom had the feeling that he was being watched. He whipped his head around.

The hall outside the door was empty.

Quickly, he replaced the sweatshirt, closed the drawer, and left the room.

Driving back to Georgetown, Tom could not push the twin images from his mind:

The lighted flag.

And the deadly weapon.

The August night was still muggy. Distant lightning flickered. Tom finally rolled up the windows and switched on the air conditioning to eliminate the heat and the stink from the befouled Potomac.

Tonight had been illuminating, in a grim sort of way. Just how emotionally stable *was* his friend?

"That's the way the movers get things done—"

Surely Senator Koop wouldn't have used his influence to get Donald a job in a delicate security operation such as Department 239-T if he had been aware of his nephew's radical leanings. On the other hand—

Tom pulled into a parking place in front of the elegant old house. A light still burned up in Cal's bedroom. He locked the car, let himself into the house, started up the stairs.

On the other hand, as Tom had recalled earlier tonight, Donald's swing to outright militancy had seemed to accelerate only after the death of his mother. Completely on his own, with no family besides the Senator, Donald was accountable to no one—except his intense and secretive friends.

Cal's door stood partially open. "Tom? It's a little late."

Tom stifled a retort and said instead, "I stopped off at Donald's. Any report from Dr. White?"

"All quiet. The mission must be proceeding according to plan."

"Cal, I—"

"What is it?"

About to enter his brother's bedroom, Tom stopped. "Nothing."

Cal appeared at the door, wearing his bathrobe. "You want to continue the college discussion?"

"Tomorrow," Tom said, heading down the hall. "I'm beat."

In his room, Tom switched on the window air conditioner and pulled off his clothes. As he headed for the shower, he realized what had stopped him at Cal's door.

A feeling of foolishness.

Surely his suspicions about Donald were just that—unwarranted suspicions. Talk of the kind in which Donald indulged had never hurt anyone, and it was most often nothing *but* talk.

And yet, the laser pistol—

A lot of people in urban areas carried weapons for personal protection, didn't they?

Yes, of course. But—*registered* weapons.

That night Tom had trouble sleeping.

4

SUSPICION

THE NEXT MORNING, the problem of Donald popped back into Tom's head. He considered it in the light of Vice-President Hand's concern about security and decided that no matter how foolish his suspicions seemed, he couldn't in good conscience keep them from Cal.

He raised the subject on the drive to Alexandria. Traffic was heavy. Heat haze obscured the horizon, promising another stifling day. Maneuvering around a slow driver, Cal laid on the horn.

"I told you I stopped at Donald's apartment last night, Cal."

"So?"

"He has some pretty strange friends. All of them are dead set against President Archibald's disarmament policies—to the point of planning a demonstration when Archibald speaks at the United Nation."

"That won't set well with Senator Koop. But it won't cost Donald his job, unless he breaks the law. The dissent trials back at the end of the Nixon administration settled that."

"But that's not the only thing."

Looking tired, Cal reached for his sunglasses. "Well, unless it's vitally important, let's skip it. There's enough to worry about with this security problem. I thought about it most of the night. Every last person in our section passed the very strictest screening before coming to work. And that includes Donald."

"Still, Donald took his tests over a year ago. Since his mother died, he's acted—well—different."

That superior tone edged Cal's voice all at once. "Can you come to the point?"

Instantly Tom felt defensive. Angry. He had an impulse to keep silent. Let Cal suffer the consequences, if any.

He couldn't do it. As Cal swung the sedan onto the beltway leading to Alexandria, Tom said, "Last night, Donald made some pretty outrageous statements. He thinks the Gate should be used for what he calls selective historical change. He'd like to see President Archibald defeated in the last election, for instance."

"I gave Donald credit for more brains."

"He doesn't understand the theory of alternative histories, I guess. Or if he does, he doesn't believe it. I tried to explain it again, but I'm no expert."

"Who is?" Cal snapped. "We're dealing with something incapable of verification except at enormous risk. Who can say how the world would have changed if Rome hadn't fallen? if Christ hadn't been crucified? if Edison had died before he found the right filament for his incandescent bulb? Would another Edison have come along? Would we be lighting our cities with gas to this day? Donald's naïve to think as he does."

"Disturbed people sometimes oversimplify things."

"I see no evidence that Donald's disturbed."

"But you hardly ever talk to him."

"Are you saying you're a better judge of character than I am?"

"I'm saying I know Donald."

"Tom, we have enough problems wrapped up in this security business without manufacturing—"

"I'm not manufacturing anything! I'm only reporting—"

"Unfounded suspicion," Cal finished. "Personally, I don't like Donald. Never have. He was rammed down my throat because of his connection with the Senator. But that doesn't alter the fact that he passed the very toughest scrutiny of his background, plus all the psychological tests."

"A lot of things can happen to a person in twelve months. Ideas—personalities can change."

"I won't argue, Tom. Do you or don't you have any concrete evidence to show that Donald represents a threat to the department?"

Suddenly Tom's forehead began to hurt. The pain was

intensified by the glare from the metal of the cars on the beltway. Why did Cal automatically sit in judgment? Why wouldn't he give others the benefit of at least feigned equality?

Tom recalled the laser pistol, started to mention it. But, noting his brother's expression, he resigned himself to silence on the subject, saying instead, "No, Cal, there's no evidence. Only Donald's talk."

"I appoint you chief monitor of everything Donald says from now on. If he tells you he's going to hop through the Gate, return to '84 and stump for President Archibald's defeat, you let me know."

Tom subsided into gloomy introspection for the rest of the trip.

Shortly they turned off the beltway. Ten minutes later, they reached the parking lot of a plain concrete building on the outskirts of Alexandria. Beside the building's tinted glass doors hung a metal plaque:

U.S. DEPARTMENT OF THE ENVIRONMENT
AIR QUALITY DIVISION

A lobby receptionist nodded good morning. They walked down a long corridor flanked by closed office doors, each with a plastic nameplate. Stopping by a door at the end, Cal took out a key. The plastic plate identified the office as belonging to Dr. Charles Q. Lind. There was no such person employed in the building.

Inside, a few pieces of furniture simulated a working office. From time to time, the papers on the desk were changed, ones with more recent dates being substituted. A folder on top showed the subject of the material to be urban pollutant emission levels.

Cal unlocked a door in the rear wall. He and Tom stepped into a private washroom of unusually large size. Alongside the medicine cabinet was a horizontal slot, wider than the usual one for used blades. Cal inserted his ident, held it there a moment, then pulled it out. Tom did the same with his card.

They stepped to the center of the floor. Suddenly a hairline crack appeared around a rectangular area. Activated by their weight, the rectangle began to sink.

In the bunker, Cal went immediately through the red door. One of the senior technicians was always on duty when a research trip was in progress, and Cal wanted to check on any overnight developments. Tom had filing to do in his brother's office. Because of security, the two girls who worked as departmental secretaries were not allowed to handle certain key documents.

Tom paused at the door of the storage rooms. Having used his own ident, Donald had already come through the bogus office upstairs, been lowered by the sinking floor, and was at work slitting open another of the costume boxes.

This morning he seemed more relaxed. He grinned, pushing his blue glasses up on his forehead.

"You should have stuck around last night, Thomas. We really hung Archy. Figuratively, of course."

"You know, Donald, if you take part in anything besides a peaceful demonstration up at the UN, you could lose your job."

"Forget it. The Senator's made that very clear. And I can't afford *not* to work here. College tuition doesn't come cheap. My friends and I are going to get Archy, all right. But in the court of public opinion. And at the polls."

For a moment Tom accepted the explanation at face value—and with relief. Then he realized how glib Donald had been.

Too glib?

Had his friend become suspicious in turn? Paradoxically, what alarmed Tom most was Donald's broad grin, so unfamiliar of late. Such abrupt changes in mood didn't seem genuine. All at once—dismally—Tom felt he was in the presence of someone he couldn't completely trust.

"When does White come back?" Donald asked.

"Nine tomorrow night."

"Cal planning to supervise?"

"Far as I know."

'I'm not signed on for duty then. Too bad. It's still kind of exciting when one of them returns."

"I'm sure Cal would clear you to come in for the arrival."

"No, I've got plans. I'll read White's monograph later."

"Okay. See you for lunch?"

Donald slid his glasses down on his nose. "Don't think so, Thomas. Unless I keep at this, I'll never finish." He turned his back.

On the way to Cal's office, Tom recalled his brother's

earlier words. Maybe Cal was right. Maybe he *was* a poor judge of character. It was a disheartening admission, because it automatically helped to validate all Cal's other attitudes and supported his contention that his decisions must be accepted without question.

Tom recalled the feeling of being watched when he discovered the laser pistol. Had one of Donald's friends passing along the hallway seen him and reported it? That would account for Donald's attempt to dismiss his own rantings as just talk.

Or was he still reading far too much into the entire situation?

Confused and feeling that he had lost another round in his long fight to establish his own competence in his brother's eyes, Tom entered Cal's office. For a moment he wanted to grab the papers to be filed and toss them helter-skelter, jumbling them hopelessly.

But he didn't.

When Department 239-T officially closed at five the following evening, Tom and Cal stayed behind. Dr. Walker went home. Dr. Stein, scheduled for duty along with Cal, said he would be back after doing a short errand.

The filing had proved a monumental task, because Tom had let it go for three weeks. He was still busy duplicating the originals on the microfiche encoder, setting up retrieval numbers for the timelock vault, and disposing of the original documents down the chute, when Cal looked in at six, suggesting that they eat supper.

Sloat's new guards were already on duty. The burly, phlegmatic-looking soldier on the far side of the thick gray door was unfamiliar.

When Tom commented on it, Cal nodded, and said, "But if Sidney Six lives up to his reputation, I'm not sure a battalion will keep him out."

They showed their idents at the cafeteria door, were admitted, and chose their food—enriched steak plus side dishes—from the cathode-ray-tube display. A smaller CRT lighted up to show the sums that would be automatically deducted from their computerized payroll accounts. In less than five minutes, wall doors popped open and extensor arms shot out the warmed trays. The department's tiny cafeteria was serviced by the larger automated installation in the Air Quality building, above ground.

As they sat down, Cal checked his watch for the second time in minutes. He was always excited when one of the researchers returned.

Tom's mind flooded with potential subjects for conversation. He really wanted to bring up the matter of Donald again, particularly the question of whether his friend shouldn't retake the psychological tests he had passed easily a year before. Then there was the question of college plans. But somehow he didn't feel up to raising either topic, only to have his views knocked down as immature and unworthy.

Toward the end of the meal, Cal said, "I thought Donald would be joining us."

"He's off duty tonight."

Cal frowned. "Last night he asked for clearance to come in. I didn't know poli sci majors were big on Roman history, but he expressed interest in getting a firsthand report on Pompeii. I okayed the request."

Puzzled, Tom said nothing.

They finished their hot vitamin drinks and left the cafeteria at five of seven.

Tom said to the guard on duty at the gray metal door, "Have you seen Koop?"

The name didn't register with the new man. Tom described him. The guard nodded.

"He came in about twenty minutes ago."

"How about Dr. Stein? Stocky man, with a beard?"

"He was back about six fifteen."

Cal slotted his ident, crossed the antechamber to the red-painted door. Tom turned off to the storage rooms. The outer door was ajar.

Inside, he flicked on the lights and looked around. No Donald. Four large costume cartons remained to be unpacked. One of them had a half-dollar-size hole punched in its side.

Returning to the antechamber, he saw the yellow warning light glowing above the door of the photo lab. The department's part-time technician was evidently readying his soup for White's film.

Five after seven. No point in heading for the Gate yet. He might as well go on with the filing—

Suddenly the red door slid back. Cal rushed across the antechamber, looking neither left nor right. Tom had never seen his brother look so worried.

Cal pressed the button that opened the gray door. "We're on alert. No one gets in or out."

The closing door hid the guard's surprised face.

"Cal, what's wrong?"

"Stein's unconscious. I think he was attacked."

Heart pounding, Tom followed his brother down the tunnel.

Dr. Stein lay sprawled in the Gate chamber, groaning. He had a nasty gash on his left temple. A thin line of blood, dry now, had run down his cheek into his beard. Rust-colored spots stained his white coat.

But those were not the only signs of trouble.

The face plate of one entire section of control equipment had been torn off. It lay twisted on the floor. In several places, the wiring in the guts of the wall had been ripped out. A smell of burned insulation clogged the air.

Tom's eyes jumped to certain dials. All red. Circuits had burned out before regulators forced auxiliary circuits into operation.

Like a hurt bear, Stein rose to hands and knees.

"Leo?" Cal said, kneeling beside him. "Can you hear me now?"

"Dizzy—" Stein shook his head with a ferocious motion. "Give me a hand up."

As he did, Cal blurted, "Who hit you?"

Dr. Stein seemed both startled and enraged as he gasped, "Koop. That kid Koop. He came in here a little while ago—I thought he was acting pretty jumpy—" He paused for breath. "Sorry. Give me a minute. I'm not exactly used to being slammed over the head."

He closed his eyes, swaying while Cal held fast to his elbow. Finally Stein signed that he could make it. Cal let go. Stein lurched to the platform and sat down. "As I said, Koop seemed to be acting strangely. But I consider that normal. Never liked him. He started asking inane questions about White's trip. I was too busy to pay much attention. I was working over there—" He pointed to an undamaged section of the wall. "I heard a sound. Didn't turn around in time. He was running at me, and he had a gun. Laser pistol, I think. He hit me with it—" Stein touched his injured temple, where an ugly bruise now showed. "I tried to grab the pistol. He kicked me in the stomach. I fell. He hit me on the head again, then gave me another kick for good measure. He went right to work—he had some kind of tool—" Quietly, Stein finished, "Somewhere in there, I passed out."

Cal had already rushed to the wall. When he turned back, his voice was full of disbelief. "The Gate's been reset."

Stein cried, *"What?"*

Cal's hand touched dials. "New spatial and temporal coordinates."

"For when?" Tom exclaimed. "And where?"

Stein waved to the exposed wiring. "Was he trying to bollix the failsafes, Cal?"

"Obviously, the crazy fool! How could he possibly believe that he could override the mechanisms locking the Gate onto Gordon's site? He's worked here long enough to know that the failsafe systems are three deep. If one's knocked out, another takes over."

"In the state Donald's been in lately," Tom said, "he probably believed he could do anything."

Almost as if he were hoping aloud, Dr. Calvin Linstrum said, "Of course we're not absolutely sure he did anything besides reset the coordinates."

"Maybe he's somewhere in the bunker," Stein said.

"Let's find out."

Cal ran down the tunnel. He returned in several minutes with grim news. "No. And the guard said Donald didn't leave by the main door."

"There's no other way out," Tom said. "Where did he go?"

"You mean where did he *want* to go?" Cal replied. "Regardless of programming new coordinates, there's only one place he could go—Pompeii. Tom, I—I'm sorry about this much. You did try to warn me. I refused to believe you—" Suddenly he raged again. "To work down here and still think he could single-handedly override—he *must* be deranged!"

"Get a reading, Cal," Stein urged. "Find out where he tried to go."

Swiftly Cal punched buttons, flipped toggle switches. Behind the curved wall, a mechanical chattering began. Shortly a paper tape fed from a slot. Cal studied the pricks in the tape.

"It makes no sense! It's programmed for a day last March."

Utter dread touched Tom. "March? What date?"

"The twelfth. What's the significance of—"

"Regardless of the significance," Stein said, "we've got big trouble. That loopy kid's running around Pompeii this minute, wearing twentieth-century clothes, flourishing a laser pistol—who knows what has already happened."

The empty, polished platform reflected the sequencing lights. Cal and Stein stared at it, as if for an answer.

All Tom could think of was the newspaper Donald had marked. A newspaper dated March 12. The weekend that President Archibald had gone into retreat in the Adirondacks—

To draft the disarmament proposals Donald Koop hated.

5

THE UNTHINKABLE

Dr. Calvin Linstrum lifted a red phone and began to dial. In a moment he said, "Arthur? This is Cal. How fast can you get down to the department? There's an emergency. I'll explain when you arrive, but I need you to monitor the Gate, perhaps all night. Right, thanks. And hurry."

"Why all night?" Stein asked when Cal hung up. He waved at one of several synchronized clocks set into the wall. "Gordon's due back in about an hour."

"I expect to meet Gordon before he returns."

"In Pompeii?" Tom exclaimed.

"Yes. I'm going back at exactly ten minutes until nine, our time. I hope to meet Gordon at his departure point. Since he can handle the language, between the two of us maybe we can catch Koop."

Dr. Stein was upset. "Cal, you're too important to the department. We can't risk losing—"

"If things get out of hand back there, Leo, there won't *be* any department. You can count on Archibald to see to that. Don't you realize that this is exactly what we hoped and prayed would never happen? You said it yourself a minute ago—imagine Donald running around the streets of Pompeii, wearing bizarre clothing, waving that laser— it's a disaster!" Again he reached for the phone. "I'll find a doctor to check on that forehead."

"Skip the doctor," Stein said. "If you're set on going

38

through the Gate, we have work to do. Costume, makeup—"

"Cal?"

His hand still on the phone, Cal turned. "Is it important, Tom?"

"I think I know the significance of the date Donald tried to program. March twelfth—" Even now, in this crisis, he found it hard to articulate the truth, because it was so frightening, so very nearly unthinkable.

Cal reacted with nervous irritation. "Tom, I have no time for speculation about—"

"It's more than speculation. I saw a newspaper Donald marked. A paper from that very same weekend." Rapidly, he reminded them of Archibald's sojourn at Camp Lookout. "Donald especially hates the President's disarmament programs. And up in the Adirondacks that weekend, Archibald began work on the proposals he's planning to present to the UN week after next."

"With a very good chance for approval," nodded Stein.

"The laser pistol he kept in his apartment"—Tom described finding it—"and the newspaper, and Donald's rantings—it all fits together. I never thought he could be that far gone, but—" The magnitude of the idea chilled him to silence.

Dr. Stein put words to it. "Attempted assassination."

Miserably, Tom nodded.

Cal's reaction was typical. "That's ridiculous."

"Don't be too sure," Stein countered. "I've noticed Koop's behavior lately. Erratic, to say the least. If he thought he could use the Gate to remove the President, a place like Camp Lookout would be an ideal spot to strike. Archibald would still be surrounded by security men, but a remote mountain camp would be infinitely easier to penetrate than the White House. There would be times when Archibald would be in the open. Coming out of the lodge to climb into his 'copter, for instance. Donald could position himself in exactly the right location. Hindsight is operating here, remember. He's probably read every published account of that weekend. And you know how a President's major movements are recorded in detail, *after* the fact. He—" Stein swallowed. "He'd have a very good chance."

For one incredible moment, Tom actually believed that his brother's stare signified furious resentment, as if Cal couldn't tolerate one of Tom's ideas being proved valid. Then, ashamed, Tom negated the thought. Cal was showing strain.

"Even if that's all true," Cal said, "it has very little to do with Donald in Pompeii."

"It has everything to do with it," Stein said. "It means Koop is most certainly deranged. We suspected it from the way he tried to override the failsafes. But this ices the cake. Donald Koop is extremely dangerous."

Silence.

Cal's shoulders sagged. Tom glanced at the clocks. Twenty-two minutes before eight. Another idea probed at the edge of his mind, refused to be stifled—

Cal started for the tunnel. "I need to tell the guard to admit Walker—"

"Cal, let me go with you," Tom said.

"Of all the nonsensical suggestions!"

The force of Cal's contempt was almost like a physical blow. But Tom kept on. "Please listen. The idea makes sense because—"

"A crisis like this—and you're thinking about *joyriding?*"

"I can *help!* I know Donald much better than you. If he's out of his head, maybe I can talk to him—keep him from getting angry—when you couldn't. Maybe I can distract him so you can get hold of the laser. You *know* how he'll react to you and Dr. White. You represent authority."

With a sinking feeling, he saw from Cal's expression that he dismissed the idea even before he said, "Impossible. I wouldn't permit—"

"I'd think very seriously about it if I were you," Stein broke in. "Sure, it's a gamble. Tom may not be any more effective than you. On the other hand, as he says, there *is* a reasonable chance that Donald might listen to him and no one else."

Bleak-faced, Cal thought it over. Tom could almost see the interior struggle, as Cal rebelled at someone else's idea. At last he said, "That would put four of us back in time at the same moment. We've never—"

"We've never faced this kind of situation!" Stein exclaimed. "You said so yourself!"

Tom asked, "If Donald really causes havoc in Pompeii, would you report it?"

"I'd be bound by conscience to do so."

"And there goes Dad's work—your work. You admitted Archibald will close the department if he finds out."

"He's right," Stein agreed. "Take him along, Cal. You'll need every bit of help you can get."

Once more Cal measured his younger brother and, Tom was sure, found him wanting. Just as Cal seemed ready to reject the plan a second and final time, he glanced at Stein. Anger simmered on the stocky scientist's face. Perhaps Stein appreicated the situation between the brothers better than Tom had ever suspected.

Finally, Cal said, "All right. But we have to hurry. We're still going through the Gate at ten minutes to nine." And he raced for the tunnel.

The next hour passed in a furious blur. Tom dashed through the bunker, gathering togas, arm rings, sandals, and makeup kit. By eight thirty he and Cal were dressed, their faces darkened with stain.

Call wanted to take person-to-person communication gear in case they became separated, so Tom hurried to the electronics stores and located two tiny talk-receive units that fitted into the special belts they wore beneath their clothing.

Both communicators had built-in recording functions. Tom recalled that he had used one of the devices at home a couple of weeks back to record one of his favorite electronic rock-pop sonatas from FM, intending to transfer it to permanent tape later. Through the unit's tiny window he saw the miniature reel still in place. He was about to remove it when Cal shouted from the antechamber, "Walker's here, Tom. Let's get moving!"

Tom left the reel in the unit and hurried down the tunnel. Both Dr. Stein and Dr. Walker were busy checking the Gate settings. Stein had slapped a bandage on his gashed temple. He seemed to have recovered. Or perhaps he was forcing himself, knowing the extreme emergency.

Tom felt odd in the thigh-length tunic of coarse, drab wool. His sandaled feet were chilly. The clock hand inched toward the hour.

At a quarter to nine, Dr. Walker asked them to step onto the platform.

Busy snapping relays, Dr. Stein nevertheless managed to say, "A pair of noble Romans if ever I saw—"

"Four minutes," Dr. Walker interrupted.

His palms itching, his stomach aching faintly—*he was*

actually going through time, back nineteen hundred and eight years—Tom tried to smile at Cal.

No response. The gold floodlights threw harsh shadows under Cal's eyes.

Tom watched the multicolored lights blinking faster and faster. Would he ever see them again? See Washington? The familiar world?

Dr. Walker barked, "Thirty seconds. Stand by."

With the minute hand at ten before the hour, the sweep second hand hit twelve. A cool, tingling darkness, enveloped Tom suddenly.

Far away, as through windy darkness, a disembodied voice seemed to call, *"Good luck—"*

There was the smell of salt wind. Feeling light-headed, Tom opened his eyes.

Something had gone wrong! Nothing but darkness—

"Cal?"

"Behind you! And don't shout. There's a cart coming."

Cal dragged Tom behind some boulders. His eyes adjusted to the deep blue night. They watched a fat grandfather pass, driving a little wagon along a road paved with large stone blocks. Two flea-bitten ponies pulled the cart, which was loaded with casks.

The road ran along the edge of the sea, at the bottom of the rocky slope where they had arrived. Beyond the road, the land dropped away to a beach. The sea murmured.

Overhead—reality was finally falling into place—stars glimmered in unfamiliar constellations. The night breeze blew balmy out of the south. At least Tom presumed the direction was south, since Pompeii was situated on ancient Latium's west coast.

The wind mingled smells of the salty ocean with another, more sulfurous tang. There was a low rumble, a tremor in the earth. The cart driver called to his nags in a strange language, urging them on.

Tom searched for the source of the rumbling, couldn't stifle an exclamation—

Vesuvio!

Its open volcanic top tinged red, the mountain rose directly behind a walled city where many lamps burned. The cart rattled away around a bend.

Cal signed for them to stand up. Tom couldn't keep his wonder-struck gaze from the city. Its buildings stretched between the foothills of Vesuvio and a wall fronting the sea. Suddenly his wonder was replaced by a grimmer thought. Tomorrow, the citizens of the Roman city would be fleeing in panic from destruction pouring out of the volcano.

"Gordon should be coming up that road any minute now," Cal said.

"Somehow I thought the Gate would transport him— and us—closer to the city."

Cal shook his head. "The Gate's accurate only within an eighth of a mile, so we have to set it for what we guess to be an open area near the destination. Besides, you can imagine what would happen if a man appeared out of the air in the center of Pompeii."

Tom followed Cal down the rock-strewn slope to the road. "Then Donald would have arrived right here?"

"Yes."

"Where do you suppose he went?"

"He'd probably head into Pompeii. There's nothing else around."

"But he'd realize he wasn't in the Adirondacks."

"Who really knows how he'd react in his state?" Cal replied.

"He has no control for the Gate."

"Right. Gordon's carrying the only one. I checked in the bunker. None of the other control units is missing. If Donald was thinking correctly, he'd have taken one for his own protection. He—Someone's coming!"

They hid behind another large stone. In a moment they saw a man approaching from the direction of the city. He seemed to be about the right height. Tom recognized White's beard, the wine-colored cloak looped across his forearm. He walked slowly, as if footsore.

Cal waited till he was ten yards away, then stood up. "Gordon?"

White's mouth rounded. He crouched as if expecting an attack.

"It's Cal and Tom."

After White recovered from the shock, he came toward them at a shuffling run. "When I heard my name in English, I thought I'd lost my mind. What's wrong, Cal? Why are you here?"

"Donald Koop used the Gate tonight. We think he's in Pompeii."

White seemed able to cope with this second shock. "I've seen no one I know—including Donald."

"You're a little late getting here. Is everything all right?"

"I'm late because checking my infernal watch requires caution. You can't just whip out a modern timepiece in public. And I did encounter one minor difficulty."

He held up his left arm. He no longer wore arm rings.

Tom noticed that White's face was bruised. "What happened?" he asked.

"Quite simply"—an attempt at a smile—"I was robbed. I dropped into a little tavern near the temple of the Fortune of Augustus—Fortuna Augusta, in the vernacular—just north of the forum, to have supper. I've picked my eating spots well until this one. No trouble. Tonight—well, every town has its criminal element. I ran into Pompeii's. They waited outside, jumped me, and stole the arm rings, plus what little money I had left. Luckily, I wasn't searched. If they'd found the control unit—" He touched his waist again. "But what about Koop? When did he arrive?"

"One or two hours ago," Tom said. "He probably disappeared into the city before you left."

White scratched his beard. "Come to think of it, there did seem to be a lot of excitement in town earlier. People congregating on street corners—I wanted to make inquiries, but I didn't. I've tried to stay unobtrusive."

"Excitement about the volcano, maybe?" Tom suggested.

Sadly, White shook his head. "Vesuvio often rumbles. The citizens haven't any idea that destruction's coming tomorrow. Oh, a few temple priests have been predicting dire things in an effort to improve public morals, but no one takes them seriously. Koop, now. Is this his idea of a lark?"

"Far from it," said Cal and explained.

"An absolute calamity!" White said at the end. "We've got to find him."

"Preferably before Vesuvio buries us all," Cal said in a somber tone.

White studied himself with one hand on Cal's shoulder while he massaged his foot. "And I thought I was done with walking. These sandals have given me blisters that you wouldn't believe."

He rubbed a moment longer, then straightened up. "The best place for information is obviously the forum. We'll have to risk speaking to someone. I've tried to keep that to a minimum, because I don't have the local dialect down pat. When my speech produces curious stares"—still limping, he started up the road, Cal and Tom alongside—"I pretend I'm a foreigner, come for a holiday. I tell them I'm from Africa. Even though it's just across the sea, it's the other side of the world."

Tom watched with awe as the lamplit city grew larger ahead of them. Outside the wall, they encountered a party of nobles, the gentlemen riding horses, the women carried in sedan chairs.

White urged his companions off the road. "Those men are *equites*. Knights. Very upper-upper. Being just ordinary citizens, we have to defer. Watch me for cues about when to get out of the way."

At the city gate, a burly soldier in armor stood under a flickering lantern. He recognized White, who whispered to the others, "This could be tricky. I came out this gate only a few minutes ago. Try to grin and act like a couple of rural clods."

Doing his best to look rustic—the effort consisted of a smile that Tom felt must appear patently false—the brothers waited while the doctor greeted the guard in Latin. The soldier scrutinized Cal and Tom. White made another remark. The guard laughed, then waved them into the city.

As they moved down a dark, twisting street, White explained, "I said you were friends of mine whom I'd planned to meet on the road. Farmers, come up from the country outside Rome. For dicing, wine—maybe a girl friend or two. That, the guard understood."

Conversation fell off. Both brothers were enthralled by glimpses of the city through which they hurried—straight, stone-paved streets; small shrines or fountains on nearly every corner; imposing houses, walls unbroken at street level except by locked gates, but opening up to spacious porches and colonnades at the second story. Nearly everywhere, the street-level walls were painted with colorful scenes of daily life. Tom remembered textbook illustrations of excavated chunks of those walls. From the paintings, archaeologists had deduced much about the ancient city.

But the walls also reminded Tom of Pompeii's doom, a doom already sealed and certain.

At this hour, most residents were indoors. From one house, laughter rang out. A dinner party? On an upper porch, a lute sang gently. The few pedestrians they met hardly gave them a glance. Presently White pointed. "The forum."

They approached a torchlit plaza some five hundred feet long and a quarter of that distance across. The forum was paved with great blocks of travertine marble, well-worn. Imposing bronze statues of gods and goddesses thrust up here and there. White enumerated some of the structures surrounding the spacious plaza. "The *macellum*—that's the local meat market. Those are shops. That small building is a temple for worship of the emperor's family."

Next he indicated a building at one end of the forum. The building was fronted by a portico and six great columns. "That's the Capitolium. A temple where you can pay your respects to Jupiter, Juno, or Minerva. Hold on—" Gripping Tom's arm, he indicated a half dozen loungers conversing near the temple steps. "You stay here, I'll see what I can find out."

White limped toward the group of citizens as Tom and Cal dropped back into the shadows of a shop portico.

White approached the citizens with his right palm upraised. The Pompeians, all rather shabbily dressed, gave him cool looks. But White maintained a friendly smile. Vesuvio rumbled. Red light washed over the statues and buildings. Then it faded.

"It seems inhuman not to tell them what's coming," Tom whispered.

Cal looked at his brother with a strange expression. "For exactly that reason, Dad very nearly destroyed all the papers in which he'd written the theoretical base of the time-phase effect. Before anyone so much as thought about constructing a Gate, he understood the agony of a situation like this."

"I didn't know. What changed his mind?"

"He was a scientist. He felt the truth couldn't be hidden, or suppressed, no matter what the consequen—Here comes Gordon."

As White limped rapidly in their direction, one of the men in the crowd stared after him, suspiciously. White darted into the portico, unsmiling. "Donald Koop is the subject of all the commotion, right enough. At least I'm reasonably sure it's Donald. It's unlikely that two—to use their words—*strangely dressed barbarians speaking a wild foreign tongue*—would appear in Pompeii on the same night."

"Have those men seen him?" Cal asked.

"No, but many others have. Apparently he made quite a stir before he was seized."

"Seized?" Tom exclaimed. "By whom?"

"The watch. According to those fellows, the watch worked up the nerve to corner Donald about an hour ago. They surrounded him and carted him off at spearpoint. For some reason, he didn't use the laser. Perhaps he was too frightened. At any rate"—White sounded despairing—"He's been imprisoned."

6

MUSIC FOR ESCAPING
FROM A ROMAN PRISON

INSTANTLY, Cal asked, "Do you know where?"

White nodded. "Just a few blocks beyond the *thermae*—the public baths. Donald's in a building where the watch collects drunks and other undesirables and holds them overnight till they can appear before a magistrate. The place is next to a baker's."

He stepped from under the portico, but Cal hauled him back. The loungers by the Capitolium steps were staring in White's direction, their expressions decidedly suspicious.

Abruptly, three of the group started walking toward the portico.

"My dialect must be showing," White whispered. "This way!"

They raced along the shadowed portico. Tom glanced back. "They're coming!"

White dashed into a sour alley between shuttered shops. Following at top speed, Tom stumbled over refuse. White signed them to the left. Distinctly, they heard the pounding sandals of their pursuers.

The three kept a fierce pace along dark streets, then finally stopped to listen.

"I think we've lost them," Cal said, breathing hard.

"There's still the problem of reaching the jail," White said. "Now it'll take longer. We'll have to circle wide around the forum."

It actually took about an hour to locate the building. They got lost twice, White failing to remember a detail of Pompeii's street geography. At last they approached a corner where a bronze fountain bubbled. White raised his hand to check their advance.

Looking both ways, he crept to the fountain. In a moment he signed them forward and pointed.

Halfway up a narrow, sloping street, a canopy supported on two poles hung over the paving stones. From the lamplit doorway drifted the aroma of hot bread. Beyond the stop a small, one-story structure showed light behind barred windows. Tom thought he heard an angry yell, though from which building, he couldn't be sure.

White said, "Let's walk past the open door of the jail and check the situation as we go by."

Doing so, they attracted no notice from the noisy bakery. Somewhere at the back, men shouted at each other in some sort of dispute.

The situation at the jail wasn't encouraging. Inside, a heavyset Roman soldier, armed with sword and spear, dozed on a stool under a lamp. He presented a direct threat to anyone attempting to sneak in by the front way.

Cal discovered a narrow passage along the far side of the jail. He darted into the passage, signaled them to wait, and disappeared.

Directly above Tom's head, a barred window shed dim light. Beyond the bars, a man sang in a low, drunken voice.

Soft footsteps alerted them to Cal's return. "Bad news. I went nearly all the way around. There's no other door."

White scowled. "Then we'll have to bring him out the main door."

"First we'd better be sure he's in there," Tom said.

Carefully, Cal reached up, grasped the lower edge of the barred window, and raised himself for a quick glance.

"He's in there, all right. With two drunks. One's asleep, the other's singing. Donald still has the laser pistol in his belt. The watch must not have recognized it as a weapon."

"All we have to do is to lure that one guard outside—" Tom began.

"It's tougher than that," Cal said. "There's a small office on the far side of the building. Through the window I saw an officer. At least he's wearing a fancier helmet than the guard is. He was writing on a tablet. We'll have to get both of them out."

"A commotion in the street?" White suggested.

"That would bring the guard. I'm not sure about the officer." Cal glanced around. "We need some kind of unusual diversion—"

Right then, Tom remembered an object concealed in the special belt. "I may have—yes. Here."

"That's only a communicator." Cal sounded annoyed.

"I was using it at home a few days ago. I returned it to the stores, but I forgot to take the reel off the playback. I recorded a rock-pop sonata. Wild stuff. Electronic. Something the Romans have never heard. We could play it full blast—"

"Just what we need," White said.

Cal chewed his lip. "Those men in the bakery would certainly come out too."

"If you can handle the first guard," White said, "I'll take care of the bakery. Then I'll come back to help with the officer. Tom, you open the cell."

"Do you suppose there's a key?"

"Probably just a bar."

"I need a weapon—" Cal prowled off down the passage, returned with a large stone. Tom's stomach tightened. He wasn't accustomed to violence. Neither were his brother and Gordon White. Their tension showed on their faces.

Tom pushed a control on the communicator, advancing the music reel to about the center. One flick of another small switch and Pompeii would be blasted with a clangorous, bleeping music that would make Roman hair stand on end. He hoped.

The three crept into the street and crossed to the far side, moving around the oblong of lamplight falling through the door. White stole down to the baker's shop as Tom and Cal recrossed to the jail, keeping to the shadows on either side of the lighted oblong. Cal flattened against the outer wall. Tom peeked at the guard.

Still dozing.

Tom bent, placed the miniaturized communicator against the worn step. He swallowed, saw Gordon White signal his readiness.

Except for the argument in the bakery, the street remained eerily still. Cal surveyed it one more time. Abruptly, he nodded.

Tom pushed the switch.

With a screech and a wheep, electronic music blared. It sounded even more cacophonous than usual through the communicator's small speaker. White kicked the poles supporting the canopy. It tumbled down over the bakery's front door.

Inside the jail, the guard let out a yell. Boots slammed on stone. A burly shadow, a man with a spear, fell across the street.

Cal edged forward. The soldier rushed through the door. Cal whipped his arm over and smacked the rock against the side of the guard's head.

Cursing, the guard dropped his spear. He staggered. Cal grabbed the spear and flung it away. From the bakery, there was louder yelling, as the bakers tried to fight their way through the canopy. White came on the run.

Enraged, the guard lurched to his feet. The earpiece of his helmet had protected him from the full force of the blow. He grabbed the hilt of his short sword. From behind, White pulled the guard's chin back, but the man was large and strong. He shook White off, leaped at Cal.

Fortunately Cal was ready. He drove his fist into the man's belly.

The punch took the wind out of the guard. White chopped the blade of his hand against the back of the man's neck. By then, Tom was through the door and racing for the jail room on his left.

Sure enough, only a bar secured the door. Tom had forgotten about the officer, though. The man came charging down a short corridor, drawing his sword.

Tom seized the nearest weapon, the guard's stool, and flung it.

The stool sent the officer reeling. By that time, White burst in the front door, followed by Cal with the rock. Tom heard sounds of scuffling and furious oaths as he yanked up the bar and hauled the screeching door open.

"Donald? Donald, come on!"

Seated against the wall, his glasses pushed up on his forehead, Donald Koop regarded Tom with a dreamy expression. A curious smile played over his lips.

All at once Donald's eyes cleared. He lurched to his feet, his expression instantly suspicious.

"Who's with you?" he demanded.

"Cal, Dr. White—What's the difference? Come on!"

"They'll just lock me up again—"

"Donald, do you know what's going to happen in Pompeii tomorrow? The volcano will erupt. The whole city will be buried! If you prefer that to getting out of here, you—" Tom held back the final words. *You must be out of your mind!*

He started dragging Donald by the arm. A couple of hard tugs seemed to restore Donald's reason. "All right. Let's go."

White and Cal had gotten the officer down on the floor. White sat on his armored chest while Cal punched his head. Three blows, and the officer was too groggy to move.

As the four plunged toward the door, Cal snatched the laser pistol from Donald's belt. About to protest, Donald suddenly wilted under Cal's furious stare.

First outside, White shouted, "Trouble!"

To the left, at the low end of the street, four soldiers appeared around the corner, a staggering man in tow. Two of the soldiers carried lanterns. Reacting instantly to the wild music, the two without lanterns pulled out their swords.

"It's the watch!" White exclaimed.

All four soldiers forgot about their inebriated prisoner and sped toward the jail.

As they began running, White shouted, "We have to reach the city gate before they do—"

Tom wondered how. The Pompeians all seemed to be powerful men. They ran at incredible speed, considering the street's upward slant. But luck worked for Tom and the rest.

It took the form of the bakers, who finally freed themselves from the canopy and rushed into the street, howling and waving their arms.

The first two watchmen collided with the bakers and tumbled. That gave Tom and the rest the needed edge.

They used it to maximum advantage, racing up the hill. Even Donald seemed aware of the danger. He kept pace.

At a corner, Tom gasped, "Cal, can't we use the Gate control from here?"

"Too risky. Keep going!"

Of the long, wild race to the gate of Pompeii, Tom remembered little, except for impressions of wall paintings streaking past the corner of his eye. White frequently led them in a new direction. Finally, a block from the gate by which they had entered, they slowed down.

Tom's chest hurt. He was sweating, dizzy. Puffing, White and Cal seemed to be in even worse shape.

"Keep walking," White wheezed, limping. "They can't be far behind."

Watching for signs of pursuit, the group reached the gate. White threw his torn cloak over Donald's shoulders, concealing the gaudy shirt and trousers as best he could. The guard didn't notice Donald until the party was directly under the lantern that hung outside the gate. Even then, his reaction was slow, for Donald was partially hidden by the others.

The guard's eyebrow hooked up, the start of a question. Behind, the watch cried warning. White and the others broke into a run.

By the time the guard yelled, they were well away from the city wall.

Tom felt he could not drive himself much farther. Even though he was in good condition, the long run had been grueling. Yet somehow he kept on. Vesuvio gave off a deep ominous sound, showing reddish light brighter than before.

As they raced around the first bend in the coast road, Cal fell. White and Tom helped him up. Cal's cheeks were pale with exhaustion. Back at the city gate, the watch appeared, swinging lanterns, and brandishing spears and swords. The party had grown to some ten men. They charged up the road at top speed.

"Get—" Cal fought for breath as they staggered on. "Get your control ready, Gordon. We have to go through the Gate the instant we reach the area—"

Of them all, only Donald Koop seemed to run without losing strength. Perhaps it was desperation, an awareness of what had almost happened to him. Ahead, Tom recognized the hillside where the Gate had deposited them earlier.

He looked back. The watch was gaining. Their lanterns bobbed wildly.

Suddenly he remembered that he had left the communicator behind, to be buried under tons of ash when Vesuvio erupted tomorrow. Would the tiny device be destroyed? Or would some archaeologist in the far future discover a melted lump of metal that, among all the other relics found in the ruins, completely defied classification?

"Can't—make it," White choked, suddenly dropping to his knees.

Panicky, Cal struggled to pull the doctor to his feet. The watch was steadily closing the distance. They would be caught, taken back—they would die in tomorrow's devastation!

Vesuvio thundered so loudly that the watch broke stride, turning their faces toward the mountain. Tom suddenly felt intense pity for the men. Doing their job tonight, they had no idea of what tomorrow held.

"Not far, Gordon," Cal gasped, supporting White. "We turn off just ahead."

The roadway shook. The red light brightened, faded. The watch resumed pursuit, but again the distraction had provided the narrow margin between capture and escape. They reached the hillside, huddling together as Cal fumbled with the small, shiny box.

He dropped it. He searched for it in the dark as Tom fought to keep from keeling over with dizziness.

Finally Cal located the box, thumbed the side. Cool, tingling darkness began to drop across Tom's mind.

He had a last vivid impression of a belch of red from the volcano. The light reflected from Donald's glasses. On the road below, a member of the watch bawled a command to halt, flung his spear—

Tom watched the spear arc through the starlight, sure it would strike one of them—

Pompeii vanished.

Exhausted, Gordon White sat on the stainless steel platform. Not looking much better, Cal stood nearby, the laser pistol in his right hand.

Tom leaned against the wall. The shock of their experience had finally hit him. Only Donald remained unmoved, seemingly nerveless.

Five minutes earlier, the four had found themselves back in the Gate chamber. A clock showed the local time as ten past one in the morning.

Cal said to Donald, "Take off those glasses. Stop hiding."

Donald obeyed, trying to smile. "Look, Dr. Linstrum, would an apology—"

"Apology! You incredible fool! Do you think words can begin to compensate for what you did? For what you *might* have done?" He indicated the gutted wall. "Repairing that damage will cost thousands of dollars. Beyond that—" For a moment, Cal couldn't go on. "You need help, Koop. Your reactions—they're simply incredible!"

Stein and Walker appeared from the tunnel. Walker carried a tray with a pot and coffee cups. The break was welcome.

Tom gulped coffee and began to feel a little better. But Cal still looked furious.

"Shall I ring up security now?" Stein asked him.

"Not till we hear his explanation. If any! You didn't expect to wind up in Pompeii, did you, Koop?"

Donald simulated embarrassment. "I admit I tried to cancel the failsafes—"

"Endangering Gordon's life!"

Donald said nothing. Tom wished he could read his friend's thoughts. He had an eerie feeling that Donald was keeping a mask carefully in place.

Finally Donald replied, "I thought I could override the failsafes without harming anyone. I've studied some electronics on my own—"

"You not only think you can play with this equipment as though it were a toy," Cal exploded, "you apparently believe you're competent to change history. Anyone who thinks that is extremely sick."

Donald let that pass, saying instead, "I'll admit I got a bad fright on that hillside when I realized where I was."

White asked, "Why did you go into Pompeii?"

"I hoped I'd find you. I was pretty scared. Not thinking clearly—"

"You make it all sound so casual! You tried to tamper with the very fabric of the past! The risks—" Again Cal bit off the words. He added, disgusted, "I honestly question whether you're sane enough to understand all I'm saying."

"Well," Donald offered, "when those watchmen caught me, I did wave the pistol at them. Thought it might scare them off—"

No one spoke. Donald finished lamely, "It didn't work."

"Did you seriously expect Roman soldiers to recognize that kind of weapon?" White demanded. "The very fact that they let you keep it should have told you—"

"I know, I know. That hit me pretty fast. Once I was in jail, I decided to use the laser to destroy the door. Late at night, when everything was quiet."

Again heavy silence. Again a weak afterthought. "I couldn't think of anything else."

Cal said, "We have a readout on the destination you tried to set on the Gate."

That, at last, produced a reaction—a visible start. Recovering quickly, Donald said, "Oh?"

"We know you were heading for March twelfth, this year. Tom told us about the newspaper you marked."

Donald glanced at Tom and Tom saw something new and terrifying in his eyes.

Hatred.

Cal was relentless. "You wanted to return to March twelfth. To Archibald's retreat in the Adirondacks. To kill him? To wipe out not only the President but his disarmament proposals?"

"Where's your proof?" Donald snarled.

"Do you deny it?" White shouted.

Blinking, Donald shriveled a little. Then he straightened up, almost proudly. "All right. I don't deny it. Archy deserves to die. He and his milksop ideals are destroying this country."

"You do need a doctor," Walker said. "The sooner, the better."

"Let's go to my office," Cal said. "I'll ring Sloat."

Walker and Stein volunteered to remain behind for a few minutes, shutting down the system. Cal gestured with the laser gun. Donald preceded him along the tunnel. Tom and Gordon White followed.

They had just cleared the red door when they heard a crash from the storerooms. White ran to the door, flung it open, froze. And Tom wondered whether his sanity had collapsed under the night's strain.

One of the costume boxes had been ripped to pieces, the contents scattered. Hovering unsupported in the air, three feet above the litter, was an incredible apparition.

It consisted of a silver metallic cube about a foot and a half square. Across its face were small dials with jiggling needles, and two rows of winking lights. From the sides of the floating box, a pair of metal stalks projected, waving gently. At the end of each glowed a hemisphere of pale green glass mounted in a metal cup.

While all their heads were turned toward the incredible sight, Donald Koop leaped.

He smashed his fist into Cal's head, knocking him sideways. Donald's fingers clawed Cal's wrist. He kneed Cal viciously. Crying out, Cal doubled over.

Donald tore the laser pistol from Cal's hand and pushed him. Cal crashed into the wall. The metal box waved its stalks in an agitated way. The green glass hemispheres pulsed with light.

Gordon White rushed forward. Donald's growl drove him back. Donald backed to the far wall, covering them with the needle-tipped gun. His glasses had fallen back into place, blue mirrors. The set of his mouth said he was desperate.

"Stand still," Donald ordered. "Otherwise I'll have to kill you all."

7

WHAT THE BOX REVEALED

Despite the warning, Tom said, "Donald, whatever you're thinking—"

"Thinking, Thomas?" A strange smile. "I'm thinking that, of all these people, you'd be the hardest to kill. But I can do it. After all, you're an Archy sympathizer. So don't force me."

White couldn't take his eyes from the floating box. "What *is* that thing?"

Donald shrugged. "I don't know. But it's obviously metal. And metal burns." He moved the laser pistol ever so slightly. "Just like the rest of you."

At this, the dials on the box jiggled more wildly. The stalks whipped back and forth. Tom had the feeling that they were suffering from a collective nightmare.

"Now listen carefully," Donald ordered. "I want you to move. But very slowly. You first, White."

"Where?"

"In there."

Their eyes swung to the thick door. Cal gasped. "The vault?"

"Don't worry," Donald told him, "I'll turn on the air supply. But I want you where you can't interfere."

"Koop, if you tamper with the Gate again—"

"Dr. Linstrum, your theories about the so-called consequences don't interest me."

"Irreparable damage to the flow of history is more than theory! It's an extremely likely possibility."

"How do you know? Who has used the Gate for anything except your stupid research? No one!"

"You can't be serious about trying to kill Archibald," White exclaimed.

His voice barely a whisper, Donald answered, "I'm an activist, not a chair-bound philosopher. I have never been more serious. Now, Dr. White—open the vault."

White shivered, walked to the massive door. He touched a button on the control panel beside the door. It swung open. White went inside.

Striding across the antechamber, Donald slid his back against the block wall directly alongside the red door. "All right, Dr. Linstrum. Open this door. Call Walker and Stein, then step back. If your face shows anything suspicious, I'll burn you first."

Fighting fear, Tom called his brother's name. A flicker of Cal's eyelids was the only sign that he had heard. Tom said, "He couldn't stop all of us if we rushed him."

Donald smiled. "I wondered when someone would think of that. Undoubtedly it's true. On the other hand, Thomas, one or more of you would certainly get killed. Would you care to sign the warrant for your brother's execution?"

Heart sinking, Tom knew Donald was right. The laser pistol could mortally injure a man in a millisecond. The risks were too great.

"Call them!" Donald commanded.

Unsteadily, Cal pressed the proper button, waited till the red metal recessed into the wall.

"Stein? Walker? Can you come here a moment?"

Donald gestured savagely. *"Back!"*

Cal obeyed. Footsteps clacked along the tunnel. Donald tensed.

The footsteps came closer. Suddenly Dr. Stein's body filled the doorway. He spotted the floating metal box, started to turn—

Dr. Walker appeared. Donald booted him in the small of the back.

Walker fell against Stein, knocking him to his knees. By the time Walker had righted himself, Donald had reached a far corner of the antechamber. His position afforded him a wider sweep with the laser.

"Don't do a thing," Cal warned Dr. Stein, as the latter struggled to his feet. "He'll kill us if you move."

"But—" Walker pointed to the metal box hovering in the storage-room door. *"What's that?"*

Suddenly Donald's eyes narrowed. "Not one of your little security devices, is it?"

Numbly, Cal shook his head. Tom was dismayed. In a thoughtless second, Cal had thrown away a prime opportunity. If they had been able to convince Donald that the box, whatever its origin, was monitoring this incredible scene—

But Cal was unskilled in deceit, unprepared, as they all were, to face this kind of situation.

Donald told Stein, "Join Dr. White in the vault. You follow, Walker."

Reluctantly, Stein obeyed. In a moment, Walker too was out of sight.

"Now you, Dr. Linstrum. Before you go in, switch on the air systems."

Cal's hand darted across the master panel. Inside the vault, ventilators whirred. Cal plodded through the door.

Once more Donald waved the laser. "Your turn, Thomas."

"Donald, listen. If you use the Gate again, you'll only land in worse trouble. Stop now and I think I can persuade Cal to give you a break—"

Wild bluff. He might as well not have bothered.

"Don't waste my time, Thomas. Inside!"

"No cause is worth—"

"Killing for?" Donald's eyes shone. "On that point, we part company. Sometimes I'm astonished that we've been friends this long. In many ways you're such a child."

Heartsick, Tom started toward the vault.

"One moment, please! What do you propose to do with me?"

Thunderstruck, Tom turned toward the metallic voice. Even Donald looked startled.

The metal box floated forward into the antechamber, waving its stalks and pulsing its green glass hemispheres. It spoke through a small grille in its lighted face. "It takes no great intelligence to deduce that whatever is happening here is against the law. I must warn you, young man—be prepared for serious repercussions. You are being observed by a member of the press."

"A member of the—" Tom began, astonished.

"I," announced the box, "am Sidney Six."

"The reporter?"

"That is correct."

Donald jumped at the box, seized one of its stalks and began pulling. "Then you go in the vault with the rest of them!"

The box couldn't offer physical resistance. But it shot its pointers to the tops of its dials, flashed its lights rapidly, and protested. "Do not think that because I am a mechanical device, I have no civil rights. It has been established in court, McElfresh versus Six, that an artificial news gathering intelligence is entitled to—*ow!*"

Flung by Donald's hand, the box sailed through the vault door and banged against the wall. It hovered unsteadily, now bobbing upward, now sinking down, while the speed of its changing lights became dizzying. Cal and the others reacted with loud exclamations.

"In!" Donald shouted, shoving Tom hard.

As Tom recovered his balance, the massive door began to close. White flung himself against the steel, tried to push it. But Donald had activated the automatic close mechanism—the shutting of the door was inexorable. Deep in its steel, relays clicked.

"I've programmed it to open in five hours," Donald called. "About daylight. By then, my work will be done."

The door shut.

White leaned against it, eyes closed. His posture summed up their defeat.

"Five hours!" Walker said. "In that time, he could destroy—"

White straightened up. "Perhaps if we made noise—"

"No use," said Cal. "There's a guard about three feet from us. But because of the bunker's design, he can't hear a thing through these walls."

"I believe I've been dented."

They all stared.

The metal box had regained its equilibrium and hovered now in front of the files that held many of Department 239-T's records. Busily, Sidney Six explored its own surfaces with its stalks. Then it rotated to show them an indentation in its case.

"See for yourselves! My editors will not take this indignity lightly. Now—" The green glass hemispheres flashed twice. "Would someone kindly explain what is going on?"

"Don't tell him—it—anything!" White warned.

"My dear sir, why not? We are in this perilous predicament together. A predicament which apparently jeopardizes the operation of your facility. Of which I have known for some time, by the way."

Cal snapped, "How?"

"Tut-tut, my dear fellow. Reveal sources? Unethical! But it's evident that matters have become quite serious. That young man with the pistol has all the mannerisms of a mental case. Since he has locked us up for the next few hours, let's have a chat."

Cal fisted his hands. "At a time like this, you want to *chat?*"

"Dr. Linstrum—naturally I know who you are—please realize that I, Sidney Six, have penetrated this installation despite your best efforts to prevent it. Your security has been breached. Therefore, I suggest you cooperate."

Perhaps it was only Tom's imagination. But the sententious metal voice suddenly sounded threatening. "Wake up, Doctor! Face reality! You no longer have any secrets from me!"

Gordon White stared at the animated box. "I thought Sidney Six was a human being."

"A frequent error, sir. However, I am no less intelligent than you. I was constructed by my news syndicate at a cost of over one million dollars. I embody the latest refinements in miniaturization, and actually represent an improvement over Homo sapiens, in that I am not subject to foolish emotional states. In that area, sir, you are the inferior."

White colored. "But I have hands. What would you say if I came over there and ripped you apart?"

"I would protest vigorously! Until you silenced my vocal mechanism, that is. Let me assure you, sir, such overreactive behavior would be futile. Another, similar device would soon be along to replace me. And I have an ace in the hole besides that. My editors have placed top priority on obtaining the story of this department. A story concealed from the public far too long."

"For very good reasons," Cal said.

"That is a matter of opinion. Oh, I am aware of your father's concern about employing your time-travel mechanism to—shall we say—tinker with the past. However, my obligation to report the facts overrides those abstruse philosophical quibbles. The public has a right to know!"

Scowling, Dr. Walker sat down on the floor. The vault's fluorescent lighting was harsh, the temperature low. But at least the ventilators supplied fresh air.

"Ahem!" said Six. "Am I to infer that the obviously unbalanced young man who forced us in here—an employee of the department, isn't he?—is Senator Koop's nephew?"

"How do you know everyone?" Stein asked.

"I have been pursuing this story for months. Ferreting out elusive leads—cryptic phrases buried in Congressional committee reports, titillating paragraphs submeged in memoranda dictated by Vice-President Hand—"

"In plain English," Tom said, "you're a spy."

"This continuing attitude of hostility is most distressing!" cried the box. "We are all in this together!"

"But you're uninvited," Cal said.

"That, of course, is true. My presence, however, is no whim of capricious fate. I laid my plans to penetrate this installation most carefully, arranging to be delivered in the latest shipment of costume cartons. From that vantage point, I intended to observe Department 239-T covertly, until I was ready to announce my presence."

Tom recalled a hole punched in one of the unpacked boxes. He mentioned it.

"Was I watching through that hole? Clever lad! Tonight I intended to emerge and explore the department. When I woke up, I assumed everyone had gone home—"

"Woke up?" Walker repeated. "Do you sleep?"

"Not exactly. From time to time I shut down to cool my circuits. When I reactivated myself, I found I hadn't reckoned on the strength of the tape with which the box was sealed. It required some effort to free myself. I had just done so when that remarkable scene took place outside. And that leads us back to Koop. I gather he plans to tamper with events in the past. What events?"

Cal seemed in more complete control now. "Don't anyone answer that ridiculous hunk of junk."

Sidney Six shot its stalks in Cal's direction. *"Ahem!* I was warned that you were an authoritarian personality, Dr. Linstrum—not to say overbearing. The warnings were not exaggerated. With only modest encouragement, I could dislike you thoroughly."

Cal shrugged. "Too bad."

"I thought you couldn't experience emotion," said Stein.

"My dislike," announced the box, "is wholly rational."

"How did you come by the name Sidney?" Walker asked.

"My editors chose it. I find it repellent, but the decision was not mine. And, taking the editorial viewpoint, I suppose one can't very well print a startling exposé under a by-line consisting of a serial number. The designation Six derives from the fact that I am of the sixth generation of constructs designed to be independent news-gathering agents. Those of us in Series Six were the first completely successful models."

"There's more than one of you?" Tom said.

"Alas, my lad, not at the moment. In a month or two, yes. Several additional Series Six models are now under construction. My earlier colleagues have been destroyed, damaged, or otherwise rendered inoperative in pursuit of journalistic excellence."

To the others, Cal said, "No wonder security had such a tough job. They were looking for a human reporter."

"Quite so! My size is extremely convenient for penetrating hidden installations and ripping off the lid of false secrecy which—"

"One more word," Cal growled, "and I'll send you to join your illustrious colleagues. In the scrapyard."

Sidney Six jiggled its dials to express annoyance. But it didn't reply.

Presently, all the humans in the vault sat down. Stein wanted to know how the box planned to escape from 239-T once its presence had been revealed.

"I mean," he said, "what's to prevent us from dismantling you?"

Sounding worried, the box replied, "When I penetrated and exposed the secret Air Force missile platforms in the Gulf of Mexico, I was similarly threatened. In such cases I strike a bargain. In return for my withholding some of the more delicate aspects of a story—I am not without a conscience, gentlemen—the operators of the facility customarily grant me the right to reveal details that will not imperil national security. As if they had any other choice! Ahem! Further, they obfuscate the intelligence authorities higher up and do not reveal my identity or nature. Everyone"—the machine flashed its hemispheres significantly—"*everyone* respects the power of the press—and of Sidney Six!"

The conversation lapsed. The chilly vault induced

lethargy, and the loquacious machine evidently ran out of things to say about itself. It did ask one or two more questions about Donald Koop's plans. Receiving no reply, it settled down to silence with its stalks folded across its lighted face.

Tom checked his watch. Fifteen past three. Donald had imprisoned them shortly before two. The lock wouldn't open until just before seven. He yawned.

Dr. Walker's chin stubble was beginning to show. Dr. Stein dozed. Cal simply sat against the wall, staring into space.

Tom let his eyes close—

He awoke at fifteen before five. He was stiff. He started to stand up.

Suddenly, as if a switch had been thrown, he *knew.*

He didn't know *how* he knew. The knowledge was simply *there,* tangled in his head along with the other certainty that he had seen President Archibald on television only four days ago.

How was it possible for him to have seen Archibald and, simultaneously, hold this other, bone-chilling fact within his mind?

"Cal?"

In Cal's horrified eyes, Tom saw that his brother shared the same terrifying knowledge. Tom forced out words. "It's the eeriest feeling—I think I know—" He swallowed. "President Archibald was killed five months ago. On the thirteenth of March. He was shot at Camp Lookout by an assassin, while he was heading for his helicopter to return to Washington. The assassin vanished in the forest and has never been caught—" Wildly, Tom stood up. "It's all there! But it wasn't in my mind an hour ago—Cal, *what's happening?*"

Cal said, "It isn't what's happening, Tom, but what *has happened.*"

Dr. Stein said, "It's as if I have an entirely new set of memories put there the moment Koop changed history. Gordon—"

"Yes," White whispered. "I know it too. God help us all."

Suddenly Sidney Six began to wave its stalks. "Archibald dead? How do you know?"

They ignored him. Walker raised a question that was deviling Tom too. "I can't figure it out, Cal. My mind tells me Archibald's gone. At the same time, I remember—vividly—that he was alive last week. Yesterday! Do we all have two sets of memories?"

A series of nods confirmed it. The sense of horror deepened.

"But how?" Stein exclaimed.

Cal answered, "I don't know."

White said, "More important—which set of memories is correct?"

Slowly, Cal raised his right hand. The index and middle fingers spread to form a V.

"Operating on the theory of alternate tracks of time, both are potentially real. Along one branch, Archibald was murdered. Along the other, he wasn't. The branch point was March thirteenth. On that day, one reality stopped—another started. Why we know about both, I'm not prepared to say. One thing's certain. There's only one reality here—" He rapped the floor. "There's one of each of us, one vault, one Department 239-T. You asked the right question, Gordon. Which reality is outside that door?"

They stared at the vault's massive portal. White said, "In two hours, we'll know."

Time crawled. Finally, the interior of the great door began to buzz and click. The thick steel swung outward.

The bunker lay empty, full of shadows. It was too early for any regular employees to have arrived for work. Stein ran down the tunnel, returned to report no sign of Donald Koop. Cal led them to his office. Sidney Six floated along behind, as if it were doing its best to remain unobtrusive. The box drifted into Cal's workroom along with the others.

Dr. Stein shut the door. Cal stepped to the telephone, seized the sculptured receiver and punched buttons.

Time seemed to stretch again. The conflicting memories buffeted Tom's mind—Archibald alive, Archibald dead—alternate time tracks—*Which was real?*

"Hello? This is Dr. Linstrum, 239-T. I'd like to speak with the President, please. Yes, thank you. Yes, I—What?" A pause. "No, don't wake him. No, let me call back in a little while. It's not that urgent."

He broke the connection, staring at them.

"The White House operator said she would connect me with President Hand."

Stein whispered, "He was sworn in after Archibald was assassinated—"

Tom knew it too. So did they all.

In a dead voice, Cal said, "So—Donald succeeded, didn't he?"

8

DARK MEMORY

Dr. CALVIN LINSTRUM ordered the red door secured and the Gate chamber declared off limits until further notice.

He, Tom, and Gordon White changed clothes. Cal sent Tom to the cafeteria for coffee and rolls.

Tom's step was slow. His mind felt mushy, and not merely from a sleepless night. As he passed the guard on duty in the corridor, he wondered what the soldier knew of Archibald's assassination. Certainly no one in the bunker save those who had been confined in the vault seemed overly upset this morning. Which present was real for them?

Returning to the department, Tom felt that his own thinking had never been so jumbled. Two sets of memories continued to conflict within him: Archibald alive and Archibald murdered, Ira Hand in office, Donald Koop at large.

At large *where?* In the Adirondacks, last March? To think of it started another headache.

As soon as Tom passed the coffee and rolls, Cal requested that his office door be locked. The department's senior technicians—White, Walker, Stein—sat or stood in postures of weariness, dejection.

Only Sidney Six, resting on a corner of Cal's worktable, seemed alert. "Is it really necessary to lock the door, Dr. Linstrum? That strikes me as a trifle melodramatic."

"I don't need advice from a tin can."

White hefted a massive paperweight. "Want me to shut the thing up, Cal?"

68

"Don't you dare!" cried the box. "I have warned you gentlemen—destroy me and another Sidney Six will very soon be manufactured to take my place. And in the event you become completely unreasonable, there is that additional ace card I mentioned. Now, I would appreciate someone giving me a summary of what has transpired. I deduce that it involves the President."

Cal's eyes narrowed. "What's his name?"

"Why, Benjamin Archibald. My memory banks—one moment." The lights on the cube flickered rapidly. "Yes, my memory banks confirm that President Archibald is alive, in office. Your remarks about contacting President Ira Hand make no sense."

"Apparently *it* doesn't have two sets of memories," Cal said to the others, ignoring Sidney Six's feverishly gyrating stalks.

"Because it's a machine?" White shrugged. "Who knows how the human mind functions under conditions like this?"

"I think it's time we called security," Walker suggested.

"In a minute," Cal nodded. "First let's make sure this new reality actually exists." He seized Sidney Six.

"Wait, wait, what do you think you're doing?"

"Putting you in that closet, Six. I'm going to bring one of my employees in here. I don't want him frightened out of his wits."

Opening the door of the combination wardrobe and lavatory, Stein stepped back. Cal shoved the box inside. It quivered its stalks in rage. "Your behavior smacks of police state brutality! I will not tolerate—"

"Stay in there and keep quiet. One squawk and I'll turn you into junk. Clear?"

The electronic journalist said, "Ahem!" But it offered no resistance.

"Leo," Cal said, "find someone out there who's just come to work. Anyone."

Dr. Stein returned shortly with a graying, slope-shouldered man who wore thick glasses.

Cal indicated a chair. "Sit down, Bigelow."

"Yes, sir, Dr. Linstrum, thank you."

"Bigelow, I want to ask you a couple of questions. You may find them peculiar. Please understand that I have good reason for asking them and don't worry too much about why." Cal did his best to sound conversational. But the shadows under his eyes belied his tension.

"Anything you say, Dr. Linstrum." Bigelow turned to White. "I came in early to make sure my soup was ready, Doctor. I thought your Pompeii film would be waiting—"

"We had an unexpected delay." White sounded vague.

Cal leaned forward. "Bigelow, do you recall what you were doing back on March 13?"

The photo technician thought a moment. "That was the day President Archibald was murdered in the Adirondacks. Sure! I remember."

"Where did you hear the news?"

"In my daughter's living room. In Richmond. My wife and I drove down for the day to visit with our grandchildren. We'd just finished dinner and little Fred was watching the television. All at once the network interrupted the movie with a bulletin. The newscaster announced that the President was dead, and that Ira Hand had already been sworn in."

Tom and the others exchanged grim glances.

"What about the assassin?" Cal asked carefully.

Bigelow hit the arm of his chair. "I'd have mobilized the whole country! I know the Government made a big effort, but they should have done more. Whoever he is, that monster should be caught! He's probably still congratulating himself. But he can't hide forever. I'll be glad when he's finally hunted down and exposed."

Shielding his eyes, Cal said, "What's your opinion of Ira Hand since he took office?"

Bigelow considered. "On the whole, good. I liked Archibald's stronger stand on disarmament. But Hand seems to have a pretty keen grasp of domestic affairs. The economy has sure boomed."

"Just one more question. What do you think of Donald Koop?"

Bigelow blinked. "The Senator's nephew? The boy who used to work here?"

"*Used* to?" Walker blurted.

"Why, you remember," Bigelow said. "He worked here all last summer. This year, the week after his college let out, he didn't show up. I heard that someone from here phoned Senator Koop and wanted to know what had happened. The Senator didn't know either. He said the boy had left his campus without explanation sometime in

March, and the Senator's been trying to trace him ever since. Some of our less responsible young people do disappear that way."

In a hollow voice, Cal said, "That's right, I was the one who called the Senator. I'd forgotten, but—now I remember."

Silence.

Bigelow shifted nervously. He had caught the peculiarity of Cal's last remark, even though its exact meaning eluded him.

Tom probed his own memory. He discovered a clear image of the morning when Donald should have returned from Harvard, but didn't. The picture was as real as the one of Donald locking them up last night. His headache grew worse.

Cal thanked Bigelow, who shuffled out. Next Cal summoned the soldier stationed outside the gray door. Cal's questions were substantially the same and the soldier's answers similar to those given by Bigelow. The soldier had been visiting a girl friend in Maryland that day in March. He had heard the news of Archibald's death on his car radio.

When the soldier had left, Cal said, "I read it this way. The memories of the other past—the one we lived through until yesterday—the one in which Archibald *didn't* die— those memories have somehow been wiped from the minds of everyone except us. I'll question a few more people, but I have a feeling we won't find the pattern any different. They remember only one past—the one in which Archibald was shot. For some reason, we remember both."

"Perhaps—" Stein sounded hesitant. "Perhaps it's because we lived through the other one. I mean, in close contact with the person who changed everything."

"Seems the only possible explanation," Cal agreed. "Those closely associated with the Gate are the only ones who can see both realities after the time track forks. My father certainly never bargained on that kind of phenomenon. Nor did I."

White said, "We do need to bring security into this."

Cal started for the closet. "Yes, but let's make sure that the news contraption will cooperate."

"I heard that!" cried a tiny voice behind the door. "Dr. Linstrum, if you continue to subject me to unjustified vilification merely because I am a mechano-electronic—"

Cal threw the door open, made a furious hooking gesture. "Come out here, Six. Shut up and listen."

The box floated into the office. Humming softly, it sank into a chair. Cal paced, spelling out in short, choppy sentences all that had taken place so far. The others were clearly worried about Cal's decision to do this. But no one interrupted. At the end, Cal gave them a hint of his reasoning when he said to the box, "Steps will have to be taken to try to undo the damage. But we can't be burdened with that job and also with trying to outwit you. So I'm offering you a choice. Give me your pledge to say nothing about what's happened, at least until we decide on the right course—" Cal's fingers closed around the same paperweight with which White had menaced the box earlier. "Or I'll smash you apart and worry about the consequences later."

"But you can't trust a—a floating tape recorder in the same way you'd trust a human being!" White protested.

"Why, he most certainly can!" Sidney Six countered. "I am not without principles. Based, of course, on a rational evaluation of the circumstances." The glass hemispheres flashed. "Obviously you face a grave predicament, Dr. Linstrum. Indeed, so does the whole country. Therefore, I will cooperate. Make no attempt to file my story—"

"Or leave this bunker."

"As you wish. Whatever the terms, I will not compound your difficulties in any way. You have my pledge, on my honor as a journalist in the great tradition of the free pr—"

"You can stow the rest," Cal sighed, returning to his desk.

But Six couldn't contain its curiosity. "President Archibald shot? President Hand in office? I have no memory of that. No memory whatsoever—until now." The stalk-tips pulsed. "Tell me frankly, Linstrum—What on earth is to be done?"

Fingers pressed to his temples, Cal said in a low voice, "That, I'm afraid, remains the question."

To confirm the theory that only those in the office were burdened with the knowledge of both time tracks, Cal questioned three more employees of Department 239-T: the two secretaries who handled correspondence and routine governmental paper work, and a man who came in regularly to service the automated cafeteria equipment. All told similar stories. Since March 13, the President of the United States had been Ira Hand.

Dr. White fell into an exhausted doze during the interrogation. Pale, Dr. Stein excused himself briefly. He looked no steadier when he returned. Toms' headache dwindled to a dull hurt. His clothing was rumpled, his hands felt gritty, his mouth tasted stale. When the questioning was over, Cal said, "As I see it—"

"If you intend to have a conference, please let me out!" complained the box in the closet. "My receptors are extremely sensitive. Continually straining them in order to hear could result in damage which—"

At Cal's wave, Tom released Six. Somewhat huffily, it announced, "I might say, Dr. Linstrum, that countless others have encountered Sidney Six with no apparent malfunction of their nervous systems. Hiding me from your employees is another gross insult."

Cal glared. The box dimmed its stalk-tips suddenly, murmured, "Ahem!" and sank to an unobtrusive spot by the baseboard.

"For the second time in twenty-four hours," Cal told them, "we need to go after Donald. This time, the stakes are much higher. Presumably he set the Gate for the twelfth of March, waited overnight until Archibald was ready to leave Camp Lookout, then pulled the trigger and fled. If we travel back to the twelfth, perhaps we can stop him."

Walker said, "You mean try to prevent the assassination before it happens? Wouldn't that be compounding the trouble? If tampering with history is dangerous, tampering twice should be doubly so."

"Unless we can simply reverse what's happened. Put things back exactly as they were by seeing to it that Koop gets nowhere near Archibald. That is absolutely all we would do—stop Koop. If the double memory effect holds true, and we succeed, we should be the only ones who'll ever know that Ira Hand was chief executive on an alternate time track. Bigelow, the guard, the rest of them—their memories should be exactly as they were—as *ours* were, yesterday, before all this began."

They agreed that it made sense. Dr. Stein asked whether Cal would clear the plan with President Hand. Cal replied that he was still mulling over that complex question. Clearly, he alone would decide.

"Actually," White said, "we have no choice as to how we use the Gate. After his experience the first time, Koop undoubtedly took a control unit. If we go anywhere, it'll be to the place and date he chose."

"You might check the control unit inventory," Cal said to Tom.

Tom returned to report, "Two gone."

"Mine," said White, "and Donald's."

"Let's make certain the Gate's locked onto the twelfth," Cal suggested. Ordering Sidney Six to remain behind, he led the others out of the office and down the tunnel. Tom was so tired, he stumbled repeatedly.

In the circular room, Dr. Stein punched up the appropriate controls. They waited for the paper tape to chatter from the slot. By the time Stein had finished running his fingers over the raised marks, he looked ill again.

"Something's wrong. The Gate's no longer set for March twelfth. I—I must be reading it incorrectly. Here, you try—" He passed the tape to Cal.

In a moment Cal's head snapped up. "It's today's date. But—he can't have done that!"

Dr. White examined the punched paper. In a voice choked with horror, he said, "The year is A.D. three thousand, nine hundred and eighty-seven!"

Tom goggled. "Two thousand years ahead? In the *future?*"

Back in Cal's office, they waited.

Dr. Stein had gone down two levels, to a section of the bunker seldom visited, in order to speed a printout of information from the Gate's internal clocks. Sidney Six, meanwhile, digested details of the latest revelation. "You mean that young lunatic has traveled into the future, as no one has done before?"

"As no one has dared to do before," Tom corrected. "A traveler in the future would face the same problem we did in Pompeii—high visibility because of the wrong clothing, unfamiliarity with the language, whatever the language will be—whatever it *is*, up ahead—"

Even attempting to speak coherently on the subject presented difficulties.

Sidney Six grasped them at once. "You used the verb *is*. Do you imply that the future coexists with the present?"

"That's a generally accepted theory of time," Cal explained. "The illustrations are numerous—a road, a river are the most common. At this point along the river of time, we exist. Five miles back, beyond a bend, let's say, five hundred years ago exists. Five miles ahead, hidden by another bend, five hundred years hence is equally real. And so, in the same way, is every other point along the river— every other moment in time in the past or future. The fact that it's beyond our power to see those past and future realities doesn't necessarily negate their existence. The complications set in when you think of dynamiting that river at a particular place, in order to rechannel the stream."

"Then you have two streams? Those alternate realities we've been talking about? Frankly, Linstrum, it's perplexing and—"

Stein burst in with a sheaf of computer printout. "It's bad, Cal."

"He's definitely gone?"

"Looks that way. The clocks show that at two thirty-four in the morning, Donald set the Gate for March twelfth, this year. He evidently returned to the chamber later. At three forty-five, the Gate was reset to the current coordinates. The temporal is exactly two thousand years in the future. The spatial is this area—Washington and vicinity. *If* it exists up there."

"Why would he go to the future?" Cal said. *"Why?"*

"If I know Donald," Tom said, "I think he might want to see the long-range results of the assassination. He'd want to know what influence on history he exerted by pulling the trigger. Beyond that, he knows forward travel is forbidden, so if he did it, he'd do it on a big scale."

"He's a madman," said White.

"It has certainly happened before," Sidney Six remarked. "Remember the Oswald affair? And the unfortunate who murdered the younger Kennedy? Such people are mad indeed. Mad with a belief in the importance of self in the scheme of human affairs. Men justify their existence in many ways, large and small. With someone like young Koop, however, the urge assumes diabolical antisocial proportions."

No one, not even Cal, reacted angrily to that, perhaps

because the hovering cube sounded almost frightened. And they knew it was right. Like Presidential assassins of the past, Donald Koop, in the name of his convictions, could both justify and carry out almost any deed.

Cal said quietly, "What a hell of a mess."

Their options had been drastically narrowed. If they went after Donald, it could only be to pursue him in A.D. 3987—a future for which they had no conceivable way of preparing. Cal's plan to prevent Archibald's murder had been destroyed at a stroke.

Stein said, "I feel as if I've been awake for years. I—" All at once, he was weeping loudly, and at the same time, apologizing, "I'm sorry—a man shouldn't—it's all been too much—I can't seem—"

On a quiet signal from White, Walker stepped forward. The two escorted Stein from the office. Tom felt only sympathy. The mind-staggering events of the night had left him in almost the same state. Cal too looked near the point of collapse. And baffled.

Cal reached for the phone. "I'm calling the President. I thought I could make a decision about Donald without consulting him. But with this new factor—"

His words trailed off. He stared at the wall in a forlorn way. Into the phone he said, "Dr. Linstrum again. This time it is an emergency."

9

DECISION

"AND THAT, Mr. President, is everything so far."

Ira Hand looked pale. He sat opposite Cal at the desk, his expression almost childlike, as if he had been handed an incomprehensible puzzle to work and could not work it.

During Cal's narration, Tom had not missed the glances between White and Walker. His brother had omitted any mention of Sidney Six. The box was once again confined to the closet, no doubt with stalks pressed against the door.

Dr. Stein was still absent, resting in the bunker's temporary sleeping quarters. Walker had given him a relaxant. Tom yawned. It was only midmorning. But he felt as though he had not slept for years.

At last, Hand spoke. "Dr. Linstrum, you confront me with facts which my mind has difficulty grasping. You say Ben Archibald was alive yesterday?"

"On one time track, yes."

"I have no memory of that. The last time I saw him was the morning last March when he departed by plane for Camp Lookout. He briefed me on a number of matters before he left. On Sunday, as he was about to enter his helicopter to fly back to the Syracuse airport, he was shot and killed. I was sworn in by the Chief Justice a few minutes after six. The next time I saw Ben, he—he was lying in state. The television coverage—the funeral—dignitaries from all over the world—surely you remember!"

"I remember very clearly. I also remember an alternate reality. There, it never happened."

Hand began walking back and forth with that characteristic rolling gait. But his step lacked energy. "You'll forgive me if I have trouble accepting your story. The death of my friend Ben Archibald was a grave loss for this nation, for the world community, and for me personally. To hear that he was *not* assassinated—"

Hand shook his head.

"Mr. President, I asked for your presence down here because there's a decision only you can make."

Hand pulled out a large handkerchief and mopped his cheeks. "Go on."

"As I said earlier, I had planned to return to Camp Lookout and try to stop the assassination. That same plan involves two steps now. First, travel to the future. There, we'd have to locate Donald, retake the control, come back here, and reset the Gate. Only then could we return to the Adirondacks."

"Travel two thousand years ahead? Doesn't the prospect alarm you?"

"Frankly, it terrifies me. But I'm willing to go. So is Dr. White. It can be argued that it might be best to leave well enough alone. On the other hand, Koop *is* in possession of the means of controlling the Gate. We can keep a constant watch on the Gate chamber, of course. But if he returns by surprise—" Cal shrugged. "Encouraged by the success of his first experiment, he might try another journey back to some other turning point in history. Very likely, if he came back to the chamber, we could stop him. But I hate to wait. Someone so unstable shouldn't be allowed to remain free any longer than absolutely necessary."

"If you should succeed in capturing Koop in the future, and if you were then equally successful in forestalling Ben's murder—I would no longer be President?"

"Nor have any memory of having been, very likely," Cal agreed. "That's why the decision must be yours. To ask a man to remove himself from the highest post in the world—"

"Ben was my great and good friend. I do not want the Presidency if the price must be refusal to try to prevent his death."

"There's no guarantee we'll succeed. All sorts of possibilities exist, including an uninhabitable earth two thousand years hence. Even if the future does prove hospitable, there's also no certainty that we can locate Koop."

Another silence. At the end, Hand said, "You must try."

Cal lost some of his tension. "Very well, sir. And thank you."

"When do you propose to leave?"

"As soon as we can. I hope this afternoon. We all need a little sleep."

"Agreed." Hand began pacing again, regaining some of his old vigor. "I also want you to take a number of steps on my behalf. One, a phone line is to be kept open between this department and my office—my bedroom if it's during the night. Regardless of the hour, I want to know the outcome."

Cal made a note. Tom thought about the results if his brother and Gordon White did succeed. Would Ira Hand suddenly cease to exist in the President's bedroom at the White House? Find himself instead in the home he occupied as second in command?

Then came another disturbing thought.

According to the river theory of time, both the March weekend and the far future coexisted right along with the present. Theoretically, Donald was in two places at once. Which Donald was real? Both?

Tom sighed. He couldn't cope with all the intricacies. Perhaps his father had been able to do so; perhaps that was why he had won the Nobel Prize.

Hand was still talking. ". . . send home all but those personnel you need to assist you in operating the Gate. I will notify Sloat that this installation is to be placed under maximum guard. I'm sure you realize that if a single word of what's happened leaked to the press and the public, we would very likely have a national crisis. No one on the outside must know!"

Cal's eyes jumped to the closet door. "Yes, sir. "Uh—naturally."

Hand started out. He turned back, no longer a supreme symbol of national authority, but simply a rather stooped, overweight man with an uncertain expression. "I still find it hard to believe. But you must do everything in your power to restore things as they were. I am not the man Ben Archibald was. We need him."

As soon as the door closed, Cal punched up the phone.

He announced over the bunker's public-address system that the department would close down in fifteen minutes, and all employees were not to return until further notice.

Dr. Walker stifled a yawn. "How about Stein?"

"If he's well enough, I'd prefer that he stay on duty. I'd like both of you to monitor the Gate."

Tom said, "What about me?"

"You heard the order."

Maybe it was Tom's tiredness. But he refused to be shunted aside. "That's not fair."

"The answer is still no." Cal rose. "Get some sleep, Gordon. I'll meet you in the ready room at three."

"Cal——" Tom began again.

"Tom, I'm in no mood for an argument!"

Temper out of hand, Tom shot back, "I'll be hanged if I'll clear out. In fact, I'm not even going to stay in the bunker. I'm going along. No, don't yell at me, Cal. Listen! You weren't in the cell in Pompeii. You didn't see Donald's reaction. At first he refused to come out. If you'd walked into that cell, he probably would have shot you. For the same reason you took me to Pompeii, you've got to take me on this trip too. You may not be able to get close enough to Donald to retake the Gate control. I can."

"You seem to forget who's in charge of this——"

A noisy thumping from the closet.

"Will someone kindly let me out? I've heard every word. And your reaction, Linstrum, strikes me as typical of your intellectual arrogance. If the lad's statements are true, his suggestion that he go on the mission is eminently sensible. Indeed—ahem! I believe I will join you myself."

"You're out of your mind!" Cal stormed when the box was out of the closet. "If you have one!"

At that, Sidney Six's green glass hemispheres lighted up. "Sir, you are continually insulting. Is that because you are afraid of losing your authority? Is that why you give free rein to your vexatious personality, constantly assuming the shrill posture of a *dictator*?"

"I'll tear you apart!" Cal shouted, lunging.

Sidney Six emitted a klaxonlike sound of alarm and sailed across the office at startling speed, eluding him. Reaching a corner, the box rose rapidly to the ceiling, then pointed its stalks at Cal. If a machine could look wrathful, this one did.

White laid a hand on Cal's arm. "We're all exhausted. Don't let your temper—"

"That—scrap heap is not going with us! Neither is my brother."

Dr. Walker looked puzzled. "Why on earth would you want to go along, Six?"

"Are you mad, sir? To view the future two thousand years hence—what a reportorial coup! Dr. Linstrum, I *insist* on accompanying you. Additionally, I insist that you permit your brother—"

"Let him speak for himself."

"Nonsense! No one can effectively speak for himself in your presence. You automatically reject any ideas that are not expressly your own. I was astonished when you deferred to Hand on the question of traveling to the future. I even imagined your character might have some redeeming qualities—"

Despite his weariness, Tom couldn't help enjoying this.

"—and further—no, sir, be quiet!" the box cried. "Do not speak until I am finished. I see I was in error. You have reverted to type. Well, sir, I not only have the desire to accompany you, I have the means to compel you to say yes."

All at once Cal stopped his attempts to reach up and seize the machine's stalks, saying, "I'm not frightened by cheap bluffs."

"No bluff, sir, rest assured. I am quite prepared to force you."

"I suppose you're going to threaten to blow the story?" Cal sneered.

"Precisely."

"You gave me your pledge—"

"Which I herewith, in the light of your overbearing manner, rescind."

Cal spun back to his desk. "I should have known better than to trust—"

"Dr. Linstrum!"

Glowering, Cal looked up.

"I have no desire to endanger national security. I fully appreciate the consequences of a security leak. Any such leak will come about as a direct result of *your* unwillingness to cooperate—*your* insistence upon playing God in each and every situation. Further, I will publicize the fact that you alone were responsible."

Cal sank into his chair, bridged his fingers in front of his nose, defensively.

"Just how do you propose to publish your story from here?" he demanded.

"You forget the principles of telemetry, sir!"

White said, "You mean you've been storing up everything?"

"Every single word I have overheard," Six confirmed. "It has all been coded—compressed—into approximately four minutes of highly sophisticated electronic signals. I have but to trigger a simple relay operation inside myself—an operation of which you will see no visible sign—and a data collection station in my editors' offices will begin to record the signals I will transmit."

"Not if I climb up there and tear you apart," Cal countered.

"By remaining close to the ceiling, I can certainly elude you for two or three minutes. By that time, the majority of data will be in the possession of my editors." For emphasis, Sidney Six flashed all its lights and quivered all its dials.

Dr. Walker couldn't hide a wary chuckle. "Score one for the machine."

White asked, "Is this the ace card you referred to a couple of times?"

"It is."

White turned to Cal. "Personally, I don't believe it's worth the risk to find out whether Six is bluffing. Besides, I'd vote to take Tom along"—Tom's spirits soared— "for the very reason he stated. I'm less enthusiastic about Six coming. The machine could be a burden."

"In a highly advanced future civilization," Six huffed, "my intellectual capacity could prove useful."

"I'm sure you believe so," White replied, with sarcasm. "Under the circumstances—being totally in the dark about what's up there—it's impossible to predict." He drew a breath. "Still, I vote to preserve security."

Cal complained, offered some additional quibbles. But the heart had gone out of the fight. And they all knew it.

Strange, Tom thought, how some nasty part of him took pleasure in Cal's defeat. Yet he didn't really enjoy seeing his brother backed to the wall.

Dr. Walker tapped his watch. "It'll be noon before we know it. If you're going to get some sleep—"

"The rest of you go ahead," Cal said, not looking up. "I have some things to organize." His hands wandered aimlessly among the papers and microfiles jumbled on his desk. The defeat by Six had cost him his pride.

With a slow step, Tom started out with the others. Six floated after them. All at once Tom grew conscious of Cal watching. He turned, and just as quickly looked away.

Tom rolled into one of the bunks in the temporary sleeping quarters. The memory of Cal's eyes haunted his mind.

Angry eyes.

Accusing.

Sidney Six might have won a small victory for itself and Tom. But in the long run, the actions of the box had only deepened the conflict between brother and brother.

Dr. Stein snored softly in the bunk across the way. The air circulators whispered. Thinking of the future, Tom imagined fantastic cities, incredibly complex machines buzzing in the skies, and on the ground—

How would the people look two thousand years hence? Physically changed, as many scientists predicted? Bodies spindly, muscles atrophied because of increased dependence on machines? And would there be that staple of stories about the future, the oversized, superintelligent head? Surely, among such people, Tom and the others would be worse anachronisms than Donald had been in Pompeii—

Donald.

Tom drifted into a doze troubled by dreams.

Sunlight flashing from his glasses, Donald toppled great gleaming towers with bursts of a laser. Superimposed like a second image in a film, another Donald crouched in powdery snow, exhaling clouds of breath, his eyes and his laser trained on a plowed area where a government helicopter whirled its rotors—

Mercifully, sleep hid the rest.

"Thirty seconds," Stein warned.

Cal, Tom, and White stood shoulder to shoulder on the platform. Clicking busily, Sidney Six floated just above them.

The humans wore neutral gray coveralls of the kind found on workmen in the bunker. All government insignia had been ripped off. Cal and White carried recorders, cameras, and weapons, concealed in the special belts under their clothes.

The neutral uniforms were the only costumes that might even come close to blending in with costuming of the far future. It was really impossible to predict what lay ahead. What if styles had changed so radically that everyone wore kiltlike skirts? Or lived in weather-controlled cities and wore nothing at all? What would they find? *What?*

"Fifteen seconds."

The lights sequenced faster. The platform vibrated.

"Ten seconds."

Though he had slept briefly, Cal still looked tired. He had wrestled unsuccessfully with the problem of spatial coordinates. There was no way to tell whether Donald Koop had set the Gate so that he, and they, would arrive in an area unoccupied by solid matter two thousand years from now. Donald had had the sense to adjust the coordinates upward, to approximately ground level. Beyond that, they could only hope.

"Five—"

The cool, tingling darkness closed around Tom.

When it vanished, he saw a world beyond all imagining.

10

A.D. 3987

THEY STOOD on a slope above a wide, eroded watercourse. In the bottom of the channel, a trickle of water gleamed with scarlet highlights. The stream looked more like oil than water. The channel twisted through a level landscape to disappear in the dull red haze of the horizon.

The fortieth century.

The wind whined. Tom coughed. The air seemed full of dust.

Their shadows stretched across what looked like burned grass. Over everything lay that dull red light.

Judging from the direction of the shadows, they were facing east. Westward, dun plains of scorched grass ran on toward the low, dark red sun. The edge of the sun was visible, though indistinct, as if screened by great clouds of dust.

Everywhere, Tom saw the same dun earth tufted with yellow grass. Could this once have been the lush Virginia countryside? What had become of the signs of civilization? Here was nothing but emptiness, a desolate uniformity, a sense of life burned out.

Waving its stalks gently, Sidney Six said, "Most remarkable!"

Cal and Gordon White headed down toward the watercourse. White pulled out his matchbox camera, put it to his eye, and clicked off exposures.

Cal said, "Either there was gross error in Donald's settings, or what's left of the Potomac has changed course considerably in two thousand years."

"How warm is it?" Tom asked. "Sixty degrees?"

"More like fifty," White replied.

Cal frowned. "Fifty? In August?"

Tom glanced at the sun. Did the masking effect of the hazy atmosphere produce the abnormally lower temperature?

"Surely there must be some human habitation—" White began.

But not another living creature, human or otherwise, could be seen anywhere in the stark landscape. At least not until Tom spotted a couple of crawling insects among the tufts of grass. He pointed them out. The others seemed reassured by the discovery. Earth, then, was not totally dead.

Sidney Six discovered the city.

It would have been easy to miss. No more than the tips of fluted towers were visible along the northern horizon. Seven or eight of them thrust up into the wan red light, glowing with dull highlights, as if they were made of glass. One tower, flared at the top, was higher than the others.

"About ten miles away," Tom guessed.

Cal shook his head. "Fifteen to twenty. Let's get moving."

They trudged straight across the desolate countryside, keeping the city as their fixed destination point. After half an hour they reached the summit of a low hill.

Still no sign of human life. But more of the city had come into view. Many shorter spires could be seen, clustering below the higher ones. Horizontal connectors—aerial roadways?—linked a number of the towers. What was disturbing about the city was its isolated quality. The travelers saw no indication of suburbs. For all its graceful, soaring beauty, the city resembled a self-contained fortress in a hostile wilderness.

They walked on. At last they viewed the city complete, and Tom realized that even those towers which seemed short were tall indeed. The lone spire soaring above all the rest had to be on the order of three hundred storys.

No one said much. Occasionally Sidney Six would clack, buzz, and talk to itself in a low tone, storing a description of the sights for retrieval later.

Obviously the residents of that city had chosen to build

upward, not outward. Because the land would not easily support life? That seemed logical, given the vegetation, the haze in the sky, the indistinct sun now half out of sight behind the western horizon.

Finally, Gordon White said, *"What's happened? This complete desolation—"*

"War?" Sidney Six suggested. "A holocaust?"

"If so, it took place a long time ago," Cal said. "There's no evidence of man-made destruction."

That was true. Yet something had caused the inhabitants of the city to abandon the land.

Tom, shivering, said, "We're assuming we'll find people in that city. What if we don't?"

White nodded. "He's right. We might be walking toward a monument."

Depressed by the thought, they trudged on.

Crossing another low rise, they started down toward what looked like another watercourse, but with two differences. No water flowed in the bottom, and it was overgrown with brown grass. At either side, low walls had been built to keep the banks from collapsing. The walls were made of blocks of a gray, stonelike material.

"Artificial," Cal said after examining the wall. "But very hard."

Walking was easier in the empty stream bed, ditch, or whatever it might be. The channel seemed to be leading toward the city. They tramped for some ten minutes. The walls, showing no evidence of disrepair, continued on either side. Suddenly they heard a low, steady moaning.

A vehicle shot into sight from around a bend, traveling fast. Streamlined, with an opaque black cowl forward, it tapered to a large exhaust tube aft. From the tube gushed a barely visible vapor. The vehicle bore cryptic markings, only one of which was familiar—a triangle, repeated twice.

The vehicle skimmed above the watercourse at a height of about two feet. But it was not a ground-effect machine riding on vertical air jets. The sere grass under its fleeting shadow showed little sign of disturbance.

"Lasers," Cal whispered.

The two men drew their weapons from under their coveralls, then hid them in large outside trousers' pockets. The speeding vehicle began to slow down. The moaning—the sound of its propulsion plant—diminished.

The vehicle came to a stop about ten feet away, then slowly descended to rest on the ground. The hinged cowl fell open. Seated one behind the other were two men.

As they climbed out, Tom caught his breath. Both were at least seven feet tall.

They were extremely slender, sticklike. Each wore a kind of dark, tight-fitting body stocking, with a hard vest over the torso. Their helmets resembled shiny black eggs. One man held a wand. A weapon?

The voice of the man without the weapon boomed through an amplifier. But his peremptory inquiry, though clear in general tone, was gibberish.

Cal waved one hand. The other was still concealed in the pocket where he had hidden the laser. "Strangers! We can't understand you."

Once more the rapid-fire gibberish crackled from the helmet. White pointed to his mouth, moved his lips, and lifted his palms in the universal gesture of noncomprehension.

The man without a weapon walked rapidly back to the vehicle. He climbed aboard and disappeared through a hatch leading to a rear compartment. When he returned, he carried a small metal wafer in one gloved hand.

The man laid the wafer against his throat and took his hand away. The wafer did not fall. Suddenly, from the amplifier, recognizable speech crackled. "We can now translate you. I am Officer Klok. Who are you?"

"Scientists," Cal said. "Travelers—"

"You are small," Klok rasped. "No people with whom we are familiar look as you do. Where have you come from?"

"We'll talk about that with whoever's in charge."

"In charge?"

"The boss. The headman." Cal gestured to the towers visible above the channel bank. "Whoever runs that city."

"The Chairman! You wish to see the Chairman?"

Strain showed on Cal's face. "Right."

"We have been observing you carefully, strangers," Klok informed them. "Since you are most odd in appearance, you will obey what we say in every respect."

"Are you police?" Tom asked.

Klok nodded. "We observed you first on the view at Central. We have come out to ascertain your nature, your origin, and your purpose in approaching Washingtowne."

"Washingtowne!" White exclaimed. "Is this the United States?"

Klok fingered the throat wafer. "I am unable to obtain a translation of those terms. This is Federal Earth, Province Amerik. You will inform us as to your purpose here."

Cal shook his head. "We'll tell that Chairman of yours, no one else."

Klok and his fellow officer conferred, Klok having removed the wafer from his throat temporarily. He replaced it after a moment.

"We will transport you. However, you are cautioned. Officer Nem has a—" The next word was unintelligible. "Arouse a commotion, or cause struggle in any way, and Officer Nem will be compelled to employ liquefaction."

"Liquefaction?" White repeated with a shudder. "No, thanks!"

"What is that device?" Klok demanded, meaning Sidney Six.

"Oh," Cal hedged, "a research machine. I told you—we're scientists."

"It jiggles its arms. It blinks its lights. It hears me?"

"I certainly do!" Six answered. "And I don't mind telling you that I find your bullying attitude highly offensive. I am a representative of the free pr—"

Noting Cal's glare of warning, the box stopped. Officer Klok, however, wasn't satisfied. "In the event of difficulties, your device is also subject to liquefaction."

"We'll keep our—ah—device under control," White promised.

Klok gestured sharply. "Inside!"

One by one they climbed into the vehicle, bent, and crawled through the hatch to the back compartment. Windowless, and so small that they had to sit hunched on padded benches along either side, the chamber smelled of citrus. The aroma came from tanks at the chamber's aft end. Fuel?"

The cowl closed. The vehicle began to vibrate. The moaning resumed. Tom felt them lift, turn, and begin to speed back up the channel toward the city.

Washingtowne. Some things had survived after all. Did the name "Federal Earth" imply worldwide government? That might be a hopeful omen.

Officer Nem pulled the hatch shut and wedged himself onto a bench foward. Because of his height, he was forced to bend almost double. But his wand, which evidently removed troublemakers by means of *liquefaction*, did not waver.

Presently, though, he seemed to relax. He unsnapped latches and lifted off his black helmet. His skull was totally hairless and gently pointed. He had alert brown eyes three inches wide.

"Mutated genetic strain?" White whispered to Cal.

Officer Nem frowned. Klok had given him the wafer, which he placed at his throat. "No speaking privately, thank you please."

"Why not?" Cal challenged.

"We do not as yet know your origin or purpose. And your appearance is suspicious in the extreme. Indeed," he added, "never in my career have I encountered persons so peculiar. Shall I not say—abnormal?"

"I guess it all depends on your point of view," White murmured, looking less than happy under the policeman's continued scrutiny.

Tom and the others were unprepared for the spectacular sight awaiting them when the vehicle landed with a gentle bump.

Officer Nem preceded them through the hatch. As Tom clambered out onto a glassy black floor, he could see little but darkness pricked by points of light. The sun had set during their trip—

Then it hit him.

The vehicle had climbed extremely high. They were looking down on the glowing tower city.

Beyond the transparent wall of a great circular room, glittering spires winked and gleamed. Tiny lights darted on the horizontal roadways below. They had arrived at the summit of the very highest tower, evidently descending through the immense, irislike port in the roof. The view was breathtaking.

Officer Klok gestured toward a moving stair. "To my surprise, the Chairman wishes to receive you personally. Step lively, thank you please."

In other circumstances, Tom might have grinned at the wafer's tangled translation. Sidney Six was muttering again, filing another description.

The moving stair was an inclined belt without steps. Tom stepped on and sank half a foot. But the belt held him comfortably after that.

On the floor below, Klok and Nem led them along a bright corridor with gleaming walls. Tom couldn't locate the source of the illumination. Around a corner, they came to imposing double doors emblazoned with a silver escutcheon incorporating images of an owl and a tree, plus an inscription in the unreadable characters Tom had noticed on the side of the police vehicle.

A muffled bell rang twice. The doors opened inward.

Inside, another huge, clear-walled chamber overlooked the city. A man rose from a curiously sculptured chair. He was even taller than the officers. A good seven and a half feet, Tom estimated, bony in the extreme. Well into middle years, the man had an austere face, and those unnerving wide eyes. One tuft of gray hair sprouted from his chin. Otherwise his head was hairless.

The man acted neither hostile nor friendly. Officer Klok made a sign of obeisance, then spoke in the unintelligible language.

The man, who was dressed in a plainly cut one-piece garment of rich purple, nodded. Then he waved in dismissal. The officers looked startled. But they marched out.

The tall man walked to the curiously designed chair. The arm contained a number of controls. He pressed a transparent button. A moment later they heard his voice. "This room is now circuited for immediate translation. No intermediary devices are required. We receive quite a few visitors from other provinces. Having the entire room wired is most helpful."

And the system was obviously more sophisticated than the wafers, Tom realized. It did a far better job of translating the man's voice into natural speech. He continued, "I am the Chairman, Doktor Phlonykus. Though I am not as suspicious as my officers—good men, those!—I might say that the room is also heavily monitored for my personal safety. In the event of any unusual activity, various concealed devices will automatically apprehend and restrain troublemakers."

Suddenly he smiled. "But I am confident such a warning is unnecessary. You do not appear unfriendly. Merely—if I will not offend you—unusual-looking. By our standards! Now, please identify yourselves."

"I'm Dr. Calvin Linstrum. You're the Chairman of this city or territory?"

"No," returned Doktor Phlonykus, "I am the Chairman of Federal Earth."

Taking a seat, he let that sink in. After a moment he continued. "Under the terms of my contract, I spend periods of one year administering affairs of the global government from each of the different province capitals. Two months ago, my daughter and I traveled here from our last residence in Europa. Normally I would not have received you in person. It was the description of your physical appearance that prompted me to do so. May I inquire where you come from?"

"From two thousand years in the past."

Doktor Phlonykus' wide lids dropped briefly over his flecked gray eyes. Tom began to catch some of the atmosphere of the room, and the city: order, control, everything in balance, in contrast to the wretched state of the surrounding countryside.

Doktor Phlonykus said merely, "Explain."

Taking the better part of an hour, Cal did.

At the end, Phlonykus said, "Your tale staggers the imagination. Please give me a few moments to adjust."

"I would have thought your society would be familiar with the principles of time travel," White said.

"I have encountered references to it in the literature," Phlonykus said. "It is mentioned in one or two obscure footnotes, if memory serves. We do not possess the knowledge of how such travel is accomplished."

Cal's eyebrows lifted. "You mean the secret's been lost?"

"Along with many other technological accomplishments of the past." Doktor Phlonykus strode to the outer wall, speaking with his back to them. "Do not let the appearance of this fine city deceive you. There are but nineteen such cities scattered around the world. And that is the entire sum and substance of Federal Earth. Ninety-nine percent of the globe has been abandoned as unfit for human life."

The travelers received this staggering news in stunned silence.

Phlonykus continued. "You say you wish assistance in locating one of your number who has journeyed to this time. The answer to that request must wait until I am convinced that you come from where you say."

"We never thought of bringing any proof," Cal admitted.

"The most convincing proofs are your own remarkable physiques. You are so short! Can the human race have changed that much in a mere two thousand years? Of course, the texts make it quite clear that it has. Yet, confronted with living examples—" Phlonykus shook his head. "I find it far easier to cope with the fact in the abstract. But now, perhaps you are in need of rest and refreshment—"

The double doors opened. A girl rushed in.

"Father, may I have permission to tap the central computation blank? My figures on the liftway stresses are wrong. The—"

She stopped suddenly, aware of the visitors.

The girl was young, about Tom's own age. Nicely built. And she was only about an inch taller than Tom. Perhaps the women in this far future had not undergone the same drastic evolutionary changes as the men.

The girl had a pretty face, with flecked gray eyes similar to those of Doktor Phlonykus, but not as wide. Judging from the way her fabric helmet fitted tightly over her head, covering it completely except for the face cutout, she was bald.

Impatiently, Phlonykus said, "Mari, I am busy conferring with these most unusual visitors—"

"I heard about them. Unusual is hardly an adequate description—" She paused. "We're being translated?"

"They do not speak our language, for reasons that I will explain later. Please state your business, Mari. Briefly!"

"My calculations have resulted in a gross error. The work crew is at a standstill. Unless I can use the computation banks tonight—"

To the others, Phlonykus explained, "My daughter is supervising construction of a new pedestrian way on the twelfth level."

"Supervising!" Tom blurted. "How old is she?"

Phlonykus replied, "In calendar years? Why, seventeen. I fail to see—"

"Seventeen and working on a building project?"

"In charge of it," Phlonykus amended. His daughter was watching Tom with unconcealed dislike. He was, after all, shorter. And he had hair.

Phlonykus told his daughter, "The name of this young

man is Thomas Linstrum. He is brother to our other visitor, just there. They do not understand our ways, Mari. I shall explain why at a more opportune time."

"The computation banks—"

"You'll have to wake a controller. However, if the crew has reached an impasse, permission is given. Next time, be more careful in preparing your theoretical base."

"Suggestion received. Thank you, Father." She started out, still studying the travelers suspiciously. "Good evening to you all—whoever you may be!"

When she was gone, Phlonykus sighed. "She is impetuous. Typical of the young. But I assure you that she has the capacity to direct the construction project. Her index number is three-ten. She is genius rated."

"Genius!" Cal cried, plainly unable to accept the idea of a seventeen-year-old girl being more intelligent than he was.

"There is nothing unusual," Phlonykus returned. "Virtually 85 percent of the children born on Federal Earth achieve that rating. As I suggested, we have lost a number of technological secrets of the past. But others have survived, including the chemical means for stimulating the human embryo and removing potentially harmful emotional factors that might inhibit the infant's development to its genetic limit. In short, we still know how to help the human brain realize its full potential."

In response to their stares, Phlonykus waved. "Chemistry, gentlemen, simple chemistry! The techniques are five centuries old! Over the short range, those techniques benefit all of society. Over the long range—" Walking slowly to the outer wall," he gazed at the lights. "It is an exercise in futility."

When he faced them again, shadows lay under his eyes. A trick of the lighting, perhaps, but appropriate to his melancholy tone. "Do not let my percentage figures concerning genius children deceive you. There is another, far more telling percentile in operation. One hundred percent of the children are born to four percent of the world's population. The rest of the race is incapable of reproducing itself. As a result, the number of human beings on the earth has been shrinking steadily for hundreds of years. Genius, in the end, will be worth nothing, since the finest brains of Federal Earth have failed to unlock the secret of how to make the race fertile again. As historical perspective, I might add that the search has been in progress literally for centuries. Without success."

Despair seemed to capture the Chairman. He continued. "In simplest terms, the race is dying. Another two or three hundred years—" He shrugged. "Very likely even the nineteen cities will be gone. Artificial production of children is not the answer. We have tried that. The same sterility to fertility ratios, ninety-six versus four, hold true among those who are laboratory-born. Indeed, recent evidence suggests that the fertile percentage may still be dropping. Sometime after your era, though not long, relatively speaking, and about nineteen hundred years before mine—"

One hand lifted, eloquent, sad.

"In a tragedy of almost unspeakable proportions, mankind destroyed itself."

11

DYING EARTH

"ARE YOU FAMILIAR with the concept of the doomsday device?" Phlonykus asked. "At least, that is what what it is called in the folklore."

Tom nodded. "People in our time speculated about it. Some kind of nuclear or chemical superweapon with the potential to destroy the earth. The idea was an extension of the arms race—bigger and bigger weapons always shifting the balance of power, until one day, some nation would construct a doomsday machine, hide it, then announce its existence—and tip the balance of power permanently toward itself. Some in our country argued for developing our own doomsday capability. But the dangers were too great. None was ever built."

"Not in your time, that's true."

"Later?" Cal said.

Phlonykus nodded. "Construction commenced after the midpoint of the twenty-first century. A one-of-a-kind project. Completion required some thirty years, due to the immense costs. And it nearly bankrupted its builders, because along with the device itself went the construction of a vast network of protective facilities. From the beginning, they meant to trigger the device. And they did."

A shudder raced down Tom's spine. "When?"

"I believe the year was A.D. 2080."

"Who built it?" White asked.

"The Asiatics, in confederation with several of the more militant nations of what was then Afrique. The device was to be used against the western nations and was eventually so employed."

Cal looked pale. "In our era, there was talk of an eventual conflict between the white race and the third world. Revenge for exploitation, real and fancied, of the latter by the former. No one dreamed it would ever come."

"Alas, it did," said Phlonykus.

Tom asked, "Was the doomsday machine a bomb?"

"Not precisely. Its heart was an installation somewhere in Asia. The exact location is documented in the histories. The control center, built around a mammoth computer, launched several dozen radiation sources in a form much like the earliest, primitive space satellites. Each orbiting carrier released intense radioactivity over a wide area of the globe. Bombs without a bang, so to speak. When the device was set off, nearly 80 percent of the human race died in a matter of days. Indeed, the builders lost much of their own population too. It simply was not possible to protect great masses of people from radiation of that high an order. As a result, Asiatic manpower was depleted far beyond the original projections. They were unable to take maximum advantage of their insane strategy. Stretched thin they were able to occupy only about half the globe for about twelve years. In truth, there was little left worth occupying."

Phlonykus paused. His voice dropped lower. "From that moment of incredible destruction dates the decline of man. For about one hundred years, the planet survived in a state close to barbarism. Young colonies on the Moon and Mars, colonies begun with high hopes at the start of the century, were cut off from contact with the mother planet. Lacking supplies, they disappeared within a generation. On Earth, the rebuilding process began—including the horrible business of rounding up the genetic freaks born as a result of the radiation. Survivors lived underground for nearly four hundred years, until the radioactive half-life decayed sufficiently to permit a return to the surface. By then, man's genetic makeup had been drastically altered. Among the side effects, the capability to reproduce was sharply curtailed. And since then, the death of the planet—and the species—has been virtually inevitable. Because it is happening so slowly—" A mournful smile. "Sometimes we pretend that all's well. But that is an illusion. Perhaps it's an illusion necessary for sanity."

Silence.

Tom gazed down into the gleaming tower city. Somewhere down there, Mari was busily supervising a construction project. To what purpose?

Could this marvelous city really represent man at the
end of his accomplishments? Recalling the wasted countryside, the city standing like a fortress in a hostile land, Tom
had a deep, sad certainty that Phlonykus was neither lying
nor exaggerating.

"As a footnote," said the Doktor, "I believe I mentioned
that during the chaotic century following 2080, many of
man's technological secrets were lost. No wonder. Entire
cities were burned by maddened mobs. Some of the
knowledge was recovered. We could once again send rockets to the Moon. But we have not done so. Far too costly.
As another example, we still know how to produce invisibility shields developed for police work in the early
twenty-first century and then adopted by the general public for personal privacy. Sometimes my officers employ
such shields. On the other hand, we know nothing of this
time-phase effect you described, Dr. Linstrum. Perhaps
now you understand my astonishment over your pursuit of
the assassin Kop."

"Koop."

"Ah, yes. You say he murdered a chief executive of
your land, one Archibeld?"

"Bald," Cal said. "Archibald."

"In our histories it has become *beld*. Faulty scholarship
after the destruction, probably."

White looked startled. "You've heard of him?"

"My dear sir, for centuries our historians have tried to
sort out the causes of the doomsday catastrophe. Your Archibeld was struck down at midpoint of his career. And I
know he worked actively on behalf of eliminating weapons
that were the forerunners of the doomsday device."

"That's why Koop killed him," Tom said. "He believed
Archibald's disarmament efforts were wrong."

"Disastrous idea! In the best judgment of our scholars,
the sudden departure of Archibeld from the world scene
centuries ago was a direct, linear cause of the arms
buildup that led to the doomsday holocaust. It is theorized
that, had Archibeld lived to carry out his plans, things
might have been entirely different—" Phlonykus gestured
toward the lighted city. "And we might not be crouching

here in our splendidly lighted caves, awaiting the final night."

"Then that makes our mission doubly important," White said.

"Wait, wait!"

They all turned, to see Sidney Six waving its stalks. "There's a logical dilemma here, Dr. Linstrum. If you apprehend young Koop, return to the Adirondack forest, and prevent Archibald's murder, time will be wrenched back on its original course—"

"And Federal Earth as we know it might well cease to exist," Phlonykus nodded. "We are, after all, the descendants—the living consequences—of Archibeld's absence from world affairs. That dilemma became apparent as we talked."

"I can't deny the possibility," Cal told him. "If we succeed, you might not be here."

"You place a high price on my help, Dr. Linstrum. To ask me to abet the possible destruction of all I have struggled to build—even the possible destruction of my self—" Doktor Phlonykus turned to stare outside, murmuring, "I am not prepared to give you an immediate answer. You must wait. You must wait."

The Chairman provided comfortable, if unusual, accommodations on a floor several levels below. One of his staff demonstrated operation of the sleeping platform, an obsidianlike slab that hung in the air with no visible means of support.

A chute whisked Tom's coverall away to clean it. Shortly, the assistant returned, reporting unhappily that the automatic cleaners had rejected the unfamiliar fabric, and consigned it to the shredder. The assistant's assistant arrived with more contemporary clothing: a balloonlike sleeping suit and, for the morning, a dark-blue body stocking much like those worn by the police.

Adjoining each private sleeping room was a small, bare chamber with a single handle jutting from the wall. Turned on, the handle activated humming sound waves that tingled Tom's bare skin and left him feeling marvelously clean.

He didn't have to adjust the lighting controls in the sleeping room. The moment he thought about darkening them, they dimmed.

He climbed onto the sleeping slab, discovering that his

body did not—could not—touch it. He was supported comfortably by the gentle currents of air.

Weary, he waited for sleep. He thought of Sidney Six, assigned its own cubicle despite its protests that it could rest its circuits anywhere, even in a hallway. He thought of Mari—

He found himself curiously interested in her.

In a girl who was *bald?*

Halfway into dreams, he laughed. With her tight-fitting fabric helmet in place, she was exceedingly attractive—

Her image vanished as he imagined silvery spheres launched into the atmosphere that day so long ago. He saw continents in flames. Hideous genetically damaged creatures roaming the land. Whole cities sunk in bunkers underground. Colonists on Mars sending messages to their home planet, then waiting, and listening to the messages dying away, unanswered—

Somewhere on this wasted planet, Donald Koop held the key to it all. The last, disturbing image in Tom's mind was of Donald, staggering over the burned landscape beneath the forlorn red sun.

He slept.

In the morning, Doktor Phlonykus summoned them to his private apartments, one floor down from the chamber in which he had received them the preceding night. A meal was ready on a triangular table. The food consisted of a colorless, tasteless beverage full of bubbles, large pink fruits resembling melons, and small dark brown loaves with a rocklike crust. Biting into the crust released a strong flavor reminiscent of yeast. In the mouth the hard substance turned chewy.

Seated on a padded bench beside Mari, Tom asked how her project was proceeding.

The flecked gray eyes regarded him with mistrust. "We have resumed schedule now that the computation error has been corrected." She ate a bite of the melon fruit. "Your name is Thomas?" She pronounced it as two distinct syllables.

"Tom," he smiled.

No smile was offered in return. "And how old?"

He told her.

"What is your intellect rating?"

He explained that, in his time, they didn't have such a rating.

"Barbaric," was her comment. It irritated him.

Doktor Phlonykus entered, looking haggard. He still wore his one-piece purple garment. Had he stayed up all night, deliberating?

Phlonykus made a few perfunctory inquiries about their comfort, then came to the point. "I have considered the matter carefully, Dr. Linstrum. Emotion argues for refusal. Reason pleads an equally eloquent case and tells me that if all the horror of the past centuries could be undone, even at a personal price that I prefer not to contemplate, I really have no choice. Therefore, I will place the full resources of my security wing at your disposal, to help you find the assassin."

Silently, three teardrop-shaped vehicles sped through the sky away from Washingtowne. It was morning, one day after Doktor Phlonykus had announced his decision. It had taken only that long to track and discover Donald Koop.

The tracking, as Phlonykus explained it, wasn't complicated. First, scanning scopes swept the surrounding area for a distance of three hundred kilometers, searching for a single bleeping dot to indicate an unusual life-form. The dot would have to be Donald, Tom learned, since wild animals were nonexistent.

Long ago, animals had become obsolete as food sources. All edibles were chemically synthesized. Insect life existed out on the barrens, to be sure. But the only surviving animal of size was a mutated variety of the dog. These were kept as pets by the city dwellers and never ran wild.

Donald, like Cal and his party, had arrived outside the limit of the short-range scanners keeping constant watch on the area immediately around the city. Cal and the others had crossed the perimeter on their way to the city, prompting the arrival of Officers Klok and Nem. Donald, on the other hand, had evidently headed in the other direction.

Following discovery of the dot, sky vehicles flew eastward at a high altitude, so Donald would not realize he was being observed. Cal was quite strong on this point. If at all possible, he wanted Donald taken by surprise. Their real goal was not Donald himself, but the Gate control.

Missing the city, as Cal and the rest had come close to doing, Donald had wandered to the shore of a dry channel that had to be the old Chesapeake Bay. No water flowed to, as Phlonykus called it, the Lantik Ocean. The Lantik was now only a hundred-kilometer-wide cesspool, roughly midway between the land masses of Amerik and Europa. Surrounding it was a vast, dusty basin.

The sky vehicles brought back high altitude holograms. An enlargement identified Donald positively. He was curled up in a posture of sleep at the top of a dune. So today, the pursuers were flying east. Two of the teardrops carried officers in black vests and helmets. The third, piloted by Phlonykus personally, had Cal and his party aboard.

Although it was early morning, the waste below looked as dim as ever. The streamlined teardrops cast lonely shadows as they ghosted along two storys above the ground.

Mari had insisted on joining them, overcoming her father's objections by saying that the construction project was now back on the track. Tom sat beside her in a sculptured seat behind the pilot's bench. He kept trying to start conversation. "For all this work you do, there must be some preparation, some schooling—"

Her wide eyes were remote. "Schooling? What is that?" Her speech sounded tinny, filtering through a throat wafer.

"A school's a place of instruction."

"An ancient concept," Phlonykus said over his shoulder. "They have not existed for centuries."

"Then how do you learn?"

"The natural way!" Mari told him. "The embryo in the mother's womb is instructed by nonvocalized electronic signals. The mind is implanted with knowledge—"

"Before birth?"

"The process is far too extensive to be completed in nine months. It is continued until age two. By that time, the infant has acquired the sum of human knowledge. Of course, learning how to apply it takes eight more years. At ten, the child is in full command of himself, has chosen his primary vocation, and is physically mature enough to begin an apprenticeship. By the end of puberty, he or she is prepared for a fully functioning role in society."

"That's incredible."

"It is your system that is incredible, Thomas. I know all about it."

When he asked how, she replied blithely that she had used a telescanning machine to read out the contents of his brain while he slept.

"Mari!" Phlonykus said. "That is hardly polite."

"No one said I could not, Father."

"And what did you find?" Tom demanded.

"That you are a very shallow person, Thomas."

He scowled.

"I am speaking intellectually, of course," she added. "Your primitive emotional makeup is quite another matter."

Across the aisle, Cal showed his dislike of the girl. He still refused to accept her supposed brilliance. For once, Tom agreed.

Mari continued matter-of-factly, "You also have peculiar notions about the female sex. As I understand it, your culture regards them as love objects."

"If you mean that we marry, have children—"

"By random chance! The dictates of the heart! To assign emotional values to a circulatory organ is most irrational. And to select a life's companion on the basis of feelings, instead of matched intellectual levels—the only word for that is still—barbaric!"

"There's a lot about us that you find barbaric, isn't there? Not to mention unpleasant."

"If you mean I am unhappy that you are here, that is true. I do not like the possibility of ceasing to exist. To surrender my life, my consciousness, so that generations in the past may labor their way forward through ignorance—"

"Mari!" Phlonykus said. "I have made the decision. Say no more."

"You may be genius rated, Mari," Tom said, "but when it comes to emotional maturity—kindness, compassion for others—you have a lot to learn."

Mari turned scarlet. Then she faced front. Her father commented, "You are wise in your own way, young Thomas Linstrum. The emotional maturity of which you speak is not arrived at by chemical means, nor at an early age. Only the experience of living can provide it."

Tom was almost mad enough to make another remark about bald girls. But he didn't. Why play her game?

A crackling sound filled the teardrop. Phlonykus threw a switch. They heard the translated voice of an officer in another teardrop. "Target in view on the screens. Range, one and a half kilometers and closing."

"Then he is still wandering the shore of the old Lantik," Phlonykus said.

"Let's not set down too closely," Cal cautioned.

The Chairman picked a landing spot half a kilometer from Donald's approximate location. The silent craft settled toward earth. With a gentle bump of extendible pads, it landed. The other two teardrops landed alongside. The party disembarked.

The wind whined as the policemen readied strange weapons that included wands, spheres, and three-pronged staffs tipped with multicolored crystals.

An officer approached. Tom recognized Klok's voice. "The target is roughly one half kilometer forward, where the ditch commences." He indicated a dune hiding the horizon.

Cal pulled his laser pistol from the belt of his dark orange body stocking. All their clothes had been demolished by the cleaning chutes. White drew his weapon too.

Sidney Six quivered its stalks. "I find this exciting. Rationally speaking, of course! Shall we go?"

"We shall," Cal nodded. "But not you."

"Dr. Linstrum, once more I protest your insufferable, authoritarian—"

Phlonykus gestured. Two officers jumped forward, wrestled the box into one of the teardrops, and locked the hatch from outside. Sidney Six complained loudly, banging the teardrop's inner wall. Finally it gave up.

"My officers will follow at a discreet distance," Phlonykus promised.

White said, "We won't call for them unless we need help."

Cal added, "The fewer of us there are, the better our chances of taking him by surprise."

An immense, stooping figure against the dull red sky, Phlonykus said, "I wish you success."

With a curt nod, Cal started up the dune.

At the top, he bellied down. White and Tom crawled up beside him. Ahead, by the drop-off at the shore of the old Bay, they saw a solitary figure.

Donald walked a few steps in one direction, then a few

steps in another. His gait was shambling, without purpose, as if his mind had abdicated all but the most primitive control—

The red sun flashed from Donald's spectacles. Cal whispered, "We'll crawl the rest of the way. Remember, he's still armed."

Tom's mouth grew dry. The wind between the dunes sang on a low, mournful note. On hands and knees, they moved forward.

12

THE BROKEN GLASSES

THEY CRAWLED to the crest of the dune separating them from Donald and the eroded shore. Sadly, Tom contrasted the picture of the Bay in his own time with the panorama of desolation confronting them now. Ghostly sand clouds blew across the basin stretching eastward. This was the end of it, then. Emptiness. Death—

Tom felt a stab of pity for Phlonykus and his people. Of what use was their technology when this emptiness was the true symbol of the destiny of man?

And Donald, with his sick, power-hungry ego, had brought the ruin.

Cal whispered, "When I signal, stand up. Don't show him your laser right away, Gordon," he added, sliding his own weapon back into his belt, the handle grip pointing forward.

"Wouldn't it be better just to charge?" White asked.

"No, we're too far away. He'd have a clear shot at us. Let's see how he reacts."

Donald was about thirty yards away, in the open. He squatted at the edge of the drop-off, drawing a pattern on the ground with the tip of his gun. His face was dreamy, self-satisfied.

"I'm glad we have some backup," White said. "All of a sudden I don't have much guts for this. Look at Koop's face. He enjoys what he sees!"

Tom looked back. Lying shoulder to shoulder on a dune, Doktor Phlonykus and a half dozen of his police awaited developments. One policeman held a rectangular device close to his helmet, as if he were watching it. Some kind of monitor screen trained on them or Donald or both?

"All right," Cal said. "Up!"

Side by side, they stood.

It took about a minute for Donald to realize that he was being observed. When he did, he jumped to his feet. The dreamy-mad smile disappeared. The red sun glared from the blue lenses.

Cal called, "Donald? We want to talk to you."

Another moment passed. Tom was conscious of their vulnerability, clear targets at the top of the dune. Donald held his laser pistol in his right hand. Tom watched for any sudden tensing of the fingers to show that Donald had decided on resistance.

Suddenly, Donald smiled. "This isn't Pompeii, Linstrum. I don't need your help."

"Donald, we want to come down there and talk—"

"Stay where you are!" Donald raised the laser. "I can hear you just fine."

Cal wiped his mouth. "All right. But please listen. There's been an emergency. We need the Gate control—"

"How do you like this?" Donald yelled, doing a crazy pirouette, a full circle, his free hand embracing the hazed sky, the blowing dust, the forlorn basin stretching eastward toward the cesspool of the Lantik. "You were all so sure that if Archy's disarmament plans failed, everything would be wiped out. Bang, no more Earth. But it's still here!"

"Doesn't he see—" Tom began.

"He doesn't see anything," White breathed. "He's lost his mind."

"It's beautiful!" Donald screamed, dancing up and down now, laughing, waving his arms. "And I made it! Me! Donald Koop!"

"If this is the Earth you made, where are the people?" Cal shouted. "Where are the cities? I'll tell you where, Donald. You wiped out almost all—"

White seized Cal's arm. "Don't anger him!"

But the damage was done.

"Don't preach at me, Linstrum! You're wrong, all of you. Archy had to die. It wasn't a catastrophe. The Earth's beautiful—and it's mine! I can do anything I want with it! *I own it!*"

Suddenly he held up a small, familiar object. "I can still change it, Linstrum. Anywhere! Anytime! I'm the *Creator!*"

Creator, moaned the echo on the wind. *Creator*—

White's cheeks shone with sweat. "No wonder he thinks it's beautiful. He believed he's the only one left. He probably never saw the city. He thinks he's—"

Unable to go on, White let an equally horrified Cal say it. "God."

In a moment, White recovered a little. "We can't handle him in that state. Signal Phlonykus."

Tom said, "I'll try to get close enough to grab the control."

"No, Tom, I forbid—"

But Tom was already starting down the dune, trying to walk slowly, steadily. The slope and the sand made footing tricky. Tom called, "Calm down, Donald. You know me."

"My friend Thomas. Sure."

"We won't hurt you, Donald. Put the gun away."

"Don't try to fool me, Thomas," Donald said. "You aren't my friend anymore. Not if you came here with them."

Tom fought his fear as he reached the bottom of the dune. "Please listen, Donald. What Cal said is true. There's been an emergency at the Gate. We desperately need the control."

Instantly, Donald pointed the laser at Tom's stomach.

"The control's mine! It's where it belongs—in the hands of the Creator! You don't realize, Thomas. I have the power of life and death now. Over *everything!*"

Donald's right hand began to shake. The laser muzzle waved erratically. "That includes you, Thomas. So stop."

He took one step back, toward the drop-off.

"I said stop right there—"

"Okay, forget the control. Let's just talk. You don't know what you've done, killing Archibald."

"I changed history!"

Tom was fifteen yards from Donald now, forcing every step. Fear consumed him. "But when you understand what's happened—"

"No closer, Thomas!"

Tom kept walking.

"I'll hurt you if you don't stop right where—*Thomas, you'd better listen!*"

Tom raised his hand. "Donald—"

From the dune, Cal shouted his brother's name. Donald's pistol hand jerked. Tom flung himself forward, hitting the sand as a thin red beam hissed through the air where he had been standing.

Someone else yelled. Tom rolled over, and saw Gordon White pitch sideways. The line of the dune top blackened with helmets. Doktor Phlonykus deployed his men right and left. Cal seemed as surprised to see the officers as Tom was.

Donald scrambled down over the edge of the drop-off, only his head in sight as he aimed the laser at the policemen running both ways along the dune, spreading out to encircle him.

"Tell them no firing!" Cal warned Phlonykus.

Donald steadied his pistol with both hands. Tom heard a wild buzz of sound, then Cal's cursing, as he smashed a three-pronged staff from the hand of the officer who had triggered it. *"I said no firing!"*

"Use the shields!" Phlonykus ordered. "That's why we brought them!"

The Chairman had wanted to employ the invisibility shields from the start. But Cal—because someone else made the suggestion, Tom was sure—had rejected the idea. Now Tom was seeing the result of his brother's stubborn insistence on controlling every situation. There was confusion—chaos—on the crest of the dune, as policemen scurried in all directions, hunting cover. Abruptly, two of them vanished, then two more, evidently employing the shields.

Tom turned again, gasped—

Donald's hands opened. The laser fell. Slowly, he sank from sight.

With the others, Tom raced toward the place where Donald had disappeared. "How is Dr. White?"

"Passed out," Cal shot back.

They found Donald at the bottom of the drop-off.

He lay on his side, his mouth open. His body bore no mark. Both blue lenses, cracked into star patterns, reflected multiple suns. He was dead.

Tom felt the beginning of tears of shock. Doktor Phlonykus said, "My men are trained to react quickly. Officer Tep would not have discharged his sonic had he not believed one of us would be hit."

Cal's weak gesture conveyed his partial comprehension of what had been a natural mistake in the tension of the moment. On his knees beside the body, he looked up all at once.

"I didn't want him dead. *I didn't want him dead.*"

"I—I'm sorry," Tom said, with difficulty. "I tried. But all at once it hit me that nobody could reason with him. He was beyond that." He shook his head. "Dr. White—"

"Mari is attending to him," Phlonykus said, reaching across to the officer holding the rectangular device Tom had noticed before. It was indeed some kind of communications monitor, with an elliptical faceplate. Phlonykus adjusted controls and said to Cal, "Had you not rejected my suggestion about the shields, Dr. Linstrum, this might have been prevented."

Still on his knees, Cal seemed not to hear.

Phlonykus scowled, then spoke to the monitor plate. "Mari?"

A colored dot pattern flashed on the plate, cleared and formed an image of the girl's face. Then the image shifted. Tom saw Dr. White lying on the sand, eyes closed.

Mari's voice rattled through the speaker. "The wound is deep, in the rib region. But it needn't be fatal."

"Take one of the craft and return him to the city at once."

Mari nodded. The image blanked out.

Cal found the control unit. Sand trickled away as he held it up. That strange, lost expression filled his eyes.

"Donald's dead. But nothing's changed. His death here didn't undo the damage."

The crushing complexity of time's paradoxes started an ache at the edge of Tom's mind. He remembered his thoughts of separate Donald's, coexisting at different points along the time river. The ache grew worse as Cal went on. "Back on that March thirteenth in the past, there must be another Donald. Still alive."

"The Donald who was there to kill Archibald?" Tom said. "*Before* he came here and—and died?"

"Yes." Hopelessly, Cal stared at the control. "We may have to capture him all over again."

Tom had no idea how long he waited. Three hours? Four? It seemed like a century.

He paced to the transparent wall, stared up at the taller

towers, blurred now as Earth's diffused sun sank. He could not stop feeling angry about the fact that, just before noon, Cal had put him down again—hard.

Why? Tom wondered again, full of the rage that had become so familiar lately. *I just wanted to go along to help him!*

It didn't help to tell himself that Cal was tense, desperately worried about the growing complexity of their predicament. Donald's death yesterday had opened a Pandora's box of new problems.

Sadness swept over Tom as he stood in a pool of weak red light falling through the tinted wall. Donald had been out of his mind toward the end. Yet Tom still remembered the good times they had shared. He thought briefly of Donald'd corpse, whisked away to refrigerated storage pending Cal's decision on disposition.

Cal's decision. Always *Cal's decision!*

Events seemed to be slipping from their collective hands. As the situation worsened, reactions grew heated—and unpleasant. If the two of them continued to exist in this state of doubt and peril, Tom's anger would surely break loose. A major blowup could be in the making.

Well, he thought, it's been coming for quite a while.

Trying to thrust the problem from his mind, Tom turned back to the shadowy room, and Gordon White.

The scientist lay in what Doktor Phlonykus called a therapy bed. It resembled a giant plastic egg sliced through its long axis. From the rim, various tubes and monitor pads ran to White's temples, arms, legs and chest. Complex equipment in the wall behind the bed read out the status of his life systems.

Directly above the bed hung a circular plate. Tiny magenta dots chased over its surface. Phlonykus had tried to explain how invisible rays from that screen healed a serious wound. But last night, when White was brought to the hospital, Tom had been too tired for much of the explanation to register.

White's color seemed good. Sleeping, he breathed regularly. A light hospital garment concealed the laser wound.

In one corner, a special communicator showed the same color image that had been visible since noon; a section of dry plain located at about the spot where they had arrived in the fortieth century. In the background, four helmeted officers lounged against the vehicle that had taken Cal and

Sidney Six to the point of departure. The officers acted restless.

The curtain of vertical light beams that served as a door dissolved. Mari walked in.

Before the light beams sprang up again, Tom glimpsed two physicians outside. One was nearly eight feet tall.

Mari's flecked gray eyes acknowledged Tom's presence before she surveyed the monitors.

"He's making excellent progress, Thomas. In fact, he may be conscious tomorrow."

"Then you're sure he'll recover?"

"As soon as your friend was safely inside this hospital, we were certain of that. The challenge has been to prevent permanent tissue damage. That, too, I'm happy to say, has been accomplished." She nodded to the communications screen with its image of the red-lighted plain. "No sign of your brother and that queer box?"

"Not yet."

He had almost grown accustomed to the rattle of her voice through the throat wafer, even begun to accept her appearance, including the tight-fitting helmet. She was a pretty girl indeed, with finely turned features, a generous mouth. What he could not grow accustomed to was her constant air of condescension. Some of this resentment showed when he said, "Shouldn't one of the regular doctors check him?"

Mari frowned. "I am fully qualified—"

"In addition to being a construction engineer, you're a practicing physician?"

"That is right."

"Well, in our admittedly primitive era, the study and the practice of medicine are complicated enough so that a man or a woman has no time for anything else. Of course, I realize you're a superior intellect—"

"But, Thomas, our staff physicians are all engaged in other fields of endeavor. Doktor Holmm, the young man you met, is also a nutritional manufacturing systems designer, as well as assistant conductor of our lightplay symphony."

"How in the name of sense can you handle so much?"

"The human mind is capable of great accomplishments, provided it is utilized to capacity. Since all of our development, learning, as you term it, is done in infancy and early childhood, there is ample time for the practice of many vocational roles."

Tom was silent. For the first time, her uncompromising stare softened a bit.

"My comments yesterday upset you, did they not, Thomas?"

"Upset me? Never."

"Speak honestly, Thomas. Perhaps I was too sharp. Now that I have grasped the limitations of your intelligence—"

"Thanks!"

"Please, I did not mean to offend—"

She looked helpless. She did have feelings after all!

Her voice dropped lower. "Before you grow angry, Thomas, consider. Despite all the accomplishments of our people, we have not found a way to arrest the dying of the race."

And she looked at him with such pain that his hostility drained away.

Mari turned back to the communicator. "How long will your brother and the reporting box be gone?"

"No way of telling. They'll have to wait for Donald to appear at Camp Lookout. And there's extra time involved, because they had to travel from here back to the Gate, in our day, to reset it for the weekend in March. Before they jump forward again, they'll have to make another stop and reset it for this present."

Sinking down in a sculptured chair, Mari said, "There is bad feeling between your brother and that chattering machine. I did not understand why your brother took it along."

Tom looked bitter. "I don't think Cal wanted to go alone. But there was another reason. Before Six got into the act, I said I wanted to go."

"And he rejected your idea?"

"Naturally. He said someone had to stay with Gordon in case the present changed suddenly, once the time flow was put back on its original course. It was only an excuse. Cal's a brilliant man. That's part of his problem. He refuses to believe anyone else is capable of coming up with good ideas."

"Especially a sibling," Mari nodded. "I detected the rivalry."

"Oh, you're a psychologist too?"

"I have taken many special seminars in intrapersonal behavior. Your brother has a weakness which is typical of men of his mental profile. It can only lead to friction, hostility—"

"There's a simpler way to say it, Mari. It can lead to trouble. And it will, unless—"

A moving image on the communicator distracted him. The brief moment of rapport with the girl was shattered.

On the screen, all four officers ran toward someone or something out of range of the lens.

Tom turned a switch, so that the officers could pick up his voice on a two-way band inside their helmets.

"Are they back?" he asked.

Alarmed, Mari pointed to the city beyond the wall. "But, Thomas—there is no change!"

She was right. If they were now on an alternate time track, no visual evidence supported the fact.

The officers had disappeared from the screen. Tom shouted. The officers heard him, dissolved the image into a distorted wide-angle view. Tom saw the policemen clustering around Cal. He glimpsed a waving stalk.

"Cal? Six? Somebody answer!"

One of the officers switched lens position again. Now Tom and Mari got a close-up of the metal box hovering. Beyond it, half of Cal's face was in sight.

Cal was unusually pale. For some reason he had his eyes closed.

"Six, did you reach Camp Lookout?" Tom asked.

"With no difficulty. Following our stop in the bunker to reset the Gate, we—I cannot report further at the moment."

"But we've waited all afternoon—"

"There is an emergency! Show him, officers!"

"They must have failed," Tom whispered.

A black helmet filled the screen. "Officer Klok requesting a therapy bed and emergency facilities. We are rushing Linstrum to the city."

A sudden shift of the lens showed Cal. In the bunker, he had evidently put on twentieth-century clothing, including an outercoat. All at once, Tom saw the reason for Cal's unsteadiness, his closed eyes.

He was in pain. A large, wet stain marked the front of his coat. A bloodstain.

Sidney Six lost its composure, exclaiming, "I suggested

treatment in our own time! From the bunker! Dr. Linstrum insisted on returning here to see what had changed. He can barely stand—"

"But who shot him?" Tom pleaded. "Is Archibald alive or dead?"

No answer. Six exclaimed, *"Catch him!"*

Cal pitched forward out of range of the lens.

13

DONALD TIMES TWO

IN A SPARSELY FURNISHED ROOM two floors below, Doktor Holmm conferred with Tom while Sidney Six hovered.

The young physician's calm manner didn't ease Tom's concern. Cal had been rushed to one of the building's surgeries. But Tom still didn't know what had happened at Camp Lookout.

Holmm said, "Your sibling's wound is classified moderately serious to serious. Transplant is the only thing."

"Transplant! What kind?"

"A portion of his intestine was nicked away by a laser. He is bleeding internally. That should be under control very shortly, however. I will perform the implantation. I would advise you to reamin here. If anxiety proves too strong, I will arrange a medication."

"You're—replacing part of his intestine with someone else's?"

Doktor Holmm paused on his way out. "Use of genuine donor's organs ceased centuries ago. We employ only the most perfect synthetics, far more durable than the human variety. What is unknown in connection with the procedure on your sibling is the possible rejection reaction of his body. We have chemical agents to offset that, of course. But metabolically, Dr. Linstrum is different from our average patient."

"What are his chances?"

"Even. It depends entirely on his reaction to the transplant. I will send someone to report as soon as we are certain."

Just as Holmm hurried out, Phlonykus entered.

"I have sent Mari to assist in the surgical theater. She will bring us word of the outcome."

Tom nodded dully, then turned to the floating box. "You and Cal failed—"

"Failed?" Sidney Six waved its stalks. "On the contrary!"

"But conditions here are just the same!" exclaimed Phlonykus. "This—time flow to which Dr. Linstrum referred has not been altered!"

"Yes it has," the machine replied. "At least I assume so, since President Archibald is alive, well, and back in the White House, where he resumed his duties on the morning of March 14, 1987."

"You found Donald?" Tom asked.

Six dials jiggled. "Most curious! Even I, with my vast ability to assimilate the unusual, have difficulty comprehending the existence of two Donald Koops. One here, another there in the Adirondacks—What? Found him? Yes. Your brother and I arrived perhaps half a mile from the site of the lodge and the adjacent helicopter landing field. Are you familiar with the terrain at the campsite?"

Tom shook his head. He had read descriptions of Camp Lookout. But in the tension of the moment, his mind was blank.

Six explained that the rambling lodge was set well back from a bluff that afforded a fine view of the mountains. The cleared landing area was located just west of the lodge, where the line of the bluff made a sweeping curve outward. Beyond the plowed ground, thick woods stretched to the bluff's edge. In those woods, deep with snow, Cal found Donald's tracks without difficulty.

Donald had built a shelter from fallen branches, about six feet back into the trees. He had a clear view of the plowed field.

"Actually," Six said, "Linstrum allowed a generous safety margin. We arrived shortly past ten on the morning of the assassination. Pardon me, the *planned* assassination. Took Koop completely by surprise. I distracted him by sounding my klaxon. Your brother leaped at him, seeking to capture the laser pistol. Unfortunately, footing was poor because of the deep snow. Your brother stumbled. Koop spun around, fired a burst. Your brother fell. Though I am sure he was in great pain, he got to his feet almost at once. Koop then aimed at the nearest target—ahem! One touch of that beam and my career would have, as it were, melted away. Before he could fire, your brother attacked him again. I assisted by flailing Koop with my stalks. He lost the laser pistol in the struggle—"

"But where is Donald now?"

"I am coming to that. My klaxon aroused the Presidential security guards. They rushed from the lodge, joined by Air Force personnel guarding the landing field. Your brother planned to render young Koop unconscious and return him to the bunker, in order to avoid lengthy explanations. Unfortunately, his wound upset those plans. Koop managed to break away and race off through the trees. Apparently he became confused about direction. We heard a piercing shriek—"

Six stopped, its green glass hemispheres flashing. "In spite of the snow, Koop was running extremely fast, you see. He burst from the trees directly on the edge of the bluff. Because of the slippery footing, he could not stop in time. He fell—"

"He's injured?" Phlonykus asked.

"He is dead."

"Dead?" Tom repeated. *"Twice?"*

"I am even less prepared to grapple with the paradoxes than you," Six admitted. "We were not able to examine the body. From the edge of the bluff, it was an exceedingly long way down to those large rocks. But he did not move. And he lay in such a curious, broken position—"

Once more Six stopped. Then, remarkably softly he said, "In the course of my journalistic endeavors, I have seen many ugly sights. But none uglier than Koop sprawled among the boulders. I believe we may safely assume that he not only died there, but on March 13, 1987, as well."

There was a strange, forlorn expression on the face of Doktor Phlonykus.

Six went on. "Dr. Linstrum found strength to return us, via the control device, to the Gate. Just in time, too. The security forces were pelting through the woods. In the bunker, I suggested immediate medical attention, as I believe I mentioned. Your brother insisted on resetting the coordinates to return us here. The rest you know. I only hope that I survive to record this remarkable story."

Tom sank down in a chair, pondering the mid-numbing paradox of two Donalds. And President Archibald restored to life—

No, wrong. Despite all the twists and turns, conditions were presumably back as they had been *before* Donald started on his disastrous time journey. The only difference was that Donald was dead—

Twice.

He heard Phlonykus say softly, "Archibeld lived?"

"Lives," Six corrected. "If I comprehend the river analogy, he lives now—this moment—back there in 1987, where he is busily promoting disarmament."

"But here, it's exactly the same!"

"I haven't had time to notice, Doktor."

Chilled, Tom stared at the Chairman. "You told us that historians considered Archibald's murder a direct, linear cause of the doomsday detonation."

"Yes."

"Perhaps all the historians were wrong."

"That begins to seem an inescapable conclusion."

"The mistake might have come from the work of just one historian, you know. One wrong conclusion, accepted by other historians for generations afterward. It's happened before. In medieval times, for instance, inaccuracies were perpetuated by scholars who assumed that some primary source was absolutely correct."

"Archibeld lived," Phlonykus repeated. "And still the doomsday spheres flew through the sky. Still the planet is dying—"

Slowly, Tom nodded. "Cal straightened out the present we live in. But yours—"

"I had such high hopes," the Chairman said. "And I am not a man who commits himself easily to emotion. You cannot grasp what I felt during the time of decision. I do not wish to die, to be wiped out by an instantaneous change in history. Yet, for the sake of others, I forced myself to permit your brother to leave, hoping"—a weary gesture— "hoping with all my heart that we would suddenly see a new Earth to replace this one that is dying. It has not happened. The historians were wrong. Completely wrong!"

The Chairman rushed from the room.

An hour passed. Two.

Tom was thinking about going to the surgery when Mari appeared. "Success, Thomas! There was no rejection. He will survive, and return to consciousness in a day or two."

Whooping, Tom hugged her.

Alarmed, she wriggled out of his grasp. Tom looked at her more closely. Her wide eyes still mirrored a deep worry.

"Mari, what's wrong?"

"It is my father, Thomas. Some terrible gloom has seized him. He has sealed himself up in his official chambers and will neither see nor speak with anyone."

The Chairman remained in seclusion for three days. Even his daughter was not permitted into his presence.

On the morning of the third day, Cal woke up. He was moved to a large room overlooking the city. The room contained two automated therapy beds. The other was occupied by Gordon White, who was up and around now. He looked sallow, but otherwise he seemed his old self.

Doktor Holmm stated that Cal would be confined for at least another week. This touched off an argument. Cal insisted that he was well. Only a sudden spasm of pain convinced him otherwise.

He fell back against the headrest, struggling to breathe. Doktor Holmm programmed a tranquilizing injection from the bed. The injection returned Cal to a drowsy state and eliminated his inclination to argue.

At dusk, Mari looked in. Relieved, she said that her father had broken his seclusion and had summoned all the chief executives of Federal Earth's nineteen cities to an emergency conference, to begin late that evening. Together with members of Phlonykus' own advisory staff, they would meet in complete secrecy. The subject of the conclave was unknown. Mari reported that her father still looked exceedingly grim.

That night, several immense airships appeared over the city. Each vessel was accompanied by a swarm of smaller protective craft. Flashing running lights of orange and green, the sky vehicles maneuvered to the summit of the tallest tower and dropped down through the iris port. The dignitaries were arriving.

Next evening, Tom discovered why.

Cal and White were finishing dinner. Cal was still in bed. White stood by the window, munching a stalklike purple fruit. Sidney Six had gone off to record its thoughts for posterity.

Abruptly, the light curtain at the door vanished. Phlonykus entered. He wore his purple garment of office, but now a silver medallion decorated the front. He looked tired, but, in contrast to the last time Tom had seen him, his step was purposeful.

"Are you up to conversing, Dr. Linstrum?"

"Of course, Doktor," Cal answered, though his voice was weak.

"My physicians say that in a day or two, Dr. White can resume normal activities. I therefore ask for his personal assistance, and permission for him to operate the Gate on my behalf."

"On your—" Cal nearly upset his meal tray. "For what purpose?"

"For the purpose of returning to the ninth day of December in the year 2080. In the archives, my research staff has discovered that, at noon of that day, the doomsday device was detonated."

All at once, they understood. White said, "You want to try to prevent it?"

"To prevent the destruction of the race? Indeed. I have outlined the potential dangers to my executives and advisers. I have particularly noted the possibility that this society may alter so radically as to cease to exist. We argued the matter more than twelve hours. The vote was narrow. Just a margin of three in my favor."

Thunderstruck, Cal began, "I don't think you understand—"

"But I do, Dr. Linstrum," Phlonykus said. Standing tall in the dim chamber, he made an imposing picture. "I permitted you to carry out your plan, hoping that it would avert the catastrophe. Now it is evident that Archibeld's role was not significant in causing—or deterring—the holocaust. It is no easier to make the decision a second time. But with the means of time control still available, I feel we must undo the damage if we can."

Cal shook his head. "The stakes are too great—"

"The stakes, my dear Linstrum, are nothing short of the survival of man. We know there is no error in the conclusion that stopping the doomsday device would reshape history as we have known it—tragically—for nineteen centuries."

Tom sensed tension in Cal's voice as he said, "I'm sorry, Doktor. The risk—"

"I am fully aware of the risk! I accept it!"

"Without my personal supervision of the Gate—"

Phlonykus snorted in contempt, more human than Tom had ever seen him. "Dr. Linstrum, you force me to remind you that your decisions are not always correct. You refused to permit my men to employ the invisibility shields in capturing Koop. In fact, you sneered at the very idea. *You* did not need such assistance."

Cal was scarlet. Phlonykus continued, "You, sir, are not the only person alive who is capable of making intelligent decisions, or managing a difficult situation through to its conclusion. I intend to go personally to 2080."

White exclaimed, "You'd endanger yourself?"

"Since the decision is mine, Dr. White, I cannot allow the danger, if any, to fall to others."

Cal's mouth wrenched. "You'd try to stop the Asiatics from detonating the doomsday machine? *In the heart of their own country?*"

"Not an easy task, I admit. But I am prepared to cope with it. Despite my age, I am in excellent physical condition. The matter of succession of authority has already been settled. Further, I can enter the past with certain advantages. The personal invisibility shields, for one. In 2080, they were in use only in western countries. They greatly improve the chances for success."

"I still can't permit you to—"

Cuttingly, Phlonykus broke in, "Are you concerned for your personal safety? Afraid you may be wiped out instantaneously?"

"My personal safety has nothing to do with it."

"Then I request—no, I demand use of the control."

"You can't demand anything!"

"If you press me, Linstrum, I can render you incapable of coherent thought. And, by means of drugs, induce Dr. White's cooperation. You are inside my city and my hospital, after all. I dislike even mentioning such measures. But if you force me—"

From the shadows, White spoke up, "As long as Doktor Phlonykus is willing to run the risks, and his own people agree—well, I think we owe him our cooperation." He faced the Chairman. "Coercive drugs won't be necessary, Doktor. I'll help you."

"Not without my authorization!" Cal raged.

Abruptly, White was at the bedside. "Cal, get hold of yourself! This man saved your life. Mine too. Without his help, Archibald would be dead. When I say we're in his debt, that's understating it!"

The tension held another moment. Then it broke, in Cal's low exhalation. "All right. Permission granted. But not until I'm recovered and can do with you."

"No," Phlonykus countered. "You will be confined for several days yet. And I intend to go as soon as possible. The mood of my executives and advisers could change. The vote could be reversed. While I have their consent, no time must be wasted."

Bitterly, Cal said, "Very well. But I don't know the whereabouts of the control unit."

"It's with the apparel we removed prior to your surgery. We have the unit in our possession. The point is, Linstrum, I could not honorably use it without your agreement. Dr. White, we shall depart as soon as I can make necessary preparations. Please see to your personal readiness."

The chairman bent toward Cal, just the merest suggestion of a bow. There was mockery in his glance, but none in his voice. "I thank you for your selfless decision."

He strode out.

A tension had been building inside Tom too. A decision. He said to White, "I'm going along. I'm sure Phlonykus will give his permission."

Before White could reply, Cal barked, "Out of the question!"

"No, Cal," Tom said, hating to do this but knowing he must. It had been a long time coming. And if ever a moment was appropriate, this one was. "I'm going to be my own man for a change. Phlonykus was right. You're a dictator."

"You're doing this deliberately, because I'm laid up in this infernal bed!"

"Partially, that's right," Tom agreed. "But I also want to help them, because they've helped us."

"I emphatically forbid you—"

"I don't care what you say, Cal. Do you understand that? I don't care. I'm grown, and I have my own mind—

regardless of what you think of it. You've pushed me to this, you know. If Phlonykus says yes, I'm going."

He spun and walked out.

In the hospital corridor, he heard Cal shouting at him to come back. He felt shaky now that it was done. And it was. In a matter of moments, the final break had come.

A break that was vitally necessary. And long overdue. But it was none the less painful for all that.

Trying to ignore the shouting, Tom walked faster.

14

"MONGOLYAH"

"JUST HERE," said the elderly technician with the wide amber eyes, "This small plate operates on a rocker principle. The pressure against the top switches on the shield. Pressure against the bottom turns it off. When the shield operates, you feel nothing. Nor is vision impaired, save perhaps for a slight blurring. Those around you are unable to see you, however, and if they are also wearing shields, you cannot see them. How is the fit?"

Tom flapped his arms. "Seems fine."

The technician moved around behind him, unfastened the straps holding the shield in place. The shield, metal but practically weightless, covered Tom's chest.

The technician placed the shield on the laboratory bench alongside the Chairman's. He said to Phlonykus, "Any other special requirements, sir?"

"Winter gear, Lexx. For myself, Dr. White, young Thomas, and Mari. I presume the journalistic box is impervious to extreme temperatures. It can accompany us if you can rig a shield for it."

"I'll try, sir." Technician Lexx's expression indicated doubt. He made notes with a light-stylus. "Cowled coats. Double thermal trousers. Boots—correct, sir?"

Phlonykus nodded. "We're going to a montainous region of the Far East. Mongolyah."

Tom didn't bother to correct the Chairman's pronunciation. He was too busy puzzling over why Mari was joining the mission—a surprise to him. It struck him as a bad idea. There would be danger enough without their being hampered by the presence of a girl.

Chagrined, he realized that he was reacting to Mari almost the way Cal had reacted to him.

Cal. He had been in Tom's thoughts almost constantly these past two days. Since the brief but bitter argument, Tom had not returned to his brother's bedside. Nor had Cal sent any messages.

Tom regretted the quarrel. Yet something in him insisted that he had no choice but to join the mission, to prove his maturity once and for all.

"Weapons, sir?" Lexx's inquiry returned Tom to the reality of the supply laboratory.

"A nerve trigger for myself and one for Dr. White," Phlonykus said. "Also as many hundred-load magazines as you can conveniently pack into the coats. Mari will want some special tools, I'm sure. But she'll tell you in person."

Lexx promised that all requisitioned items would be ready on time. Departure was scheduled in about forty-eight hours, following a final, exhaustive physical checkup for Gordon White, to make sure he was fit for the ordeal.

Phlonykus piloted the sleek vehicle that bore them across the traffic ways toward the tallest tower. Tom asked, "When did your daughter decide to come with us?"

"I made the decision, Thomas. We needed someone to disarm the doomsday device. From what Mari has learned in the archives, she assures me it will be a simple task. All the pads that launched the radiation bearers were operated from one computer—a computer complex for its day, but primitive by our standards. According to Mari, one hundred and forty-four reprogramming steps will totally disarm the system, and cause it to burn itself out beyond repair."

Tom grinned. "I hope she brings a list."

"Oh, no," Phlonykus returned matter-of-factly. "She will have it all in her head, in perfect sequence." He noticed Tom's expression, and smiled. "You continue to find Mari's abilities unusual, don't you?"

"That's an understatement, sir."

"But disarming the computer will be childishly easy! No more difficult for Mari than it would be for a person of your era to repair a wooden wheel. Knowledge is relative to the task. To Mari, that computer is a nineteen-hundred-year-old antique. You should not feel intimidated—or inferior."

"I shouldn't. But I do."

But there was another reason he wished she were not going along, Tom admitted to himself. He was worried about her safety.

It was startling to realize that, against all odds, he had grown to like her. Probably in part because she represented a challenge. But on another level, he simply found her very attractive.

The Chairman steered the cab through a port in the side of the tall tower. Automatic controls braked the vehicle against a landing platform.

As they walked to the moving stair, the Chairman asked, "Have you visited your brother today? He is making excellent progress."

"I'm glad to hear that. I haven't seen him."

"Do you intend to see him before departure?"

"I suppose I'll have to."

"This gulf between you is an unhappy thing."

Tom tried to shrug it off. "He thinks I'm a child."

"Do you really wish to risk your life in Mongolyah to prove otherwise?"

Tom looked into Phlonykus' strange wide eyes. "Yes."

Frowning, the Chairman studied the reflective walls beside the slowly ascending belt. He said at last, "Given Dr. Linstrum's attitudes, I suppose that is the only possible answer."

Some three dozen bald, emaciated dignitaries accompanied the party to the departure site two days later. Tom presumed the men must be the Chairman's advisers. Black-helmeted officers formed a protective ring around them.

Sidney Six had come along, waving its stalks as it protested Phlonykus' decision that it be left behind. "Arbitrary! As arbitrary as Linstrum, if not more so—ahem!" Technician Lexx had failed to adapt an invisibility shield to fit the metal box.

Tom, Phlonykus, Mari, and White stood apart from the rest. They were leaving from approximately the same spot at which Tom and his companions had arrived. Tom could hardly move inside his heavy trousers and cowled, fur-lined coat. The garments smelled musty, as though retrieved from some museum.

Doktor Phlonykus raised his gloved hand. "I wish you well. May we all be reunited in a happier present."

Confusing thoughts flooded Tom's mind in these last moments. He felt a keen regret that Cal was not well enough to be returned to the bunker. If Mari succeeded, if history changed, would Cal still be in the hospital here? Would *here* exist?

Earlier, Tom had visited his brother in his recovery room. They had exchanged little more than curt good-bys. Cal's expression remained almost childishly sullen. Tom wondered how he could despise his brother's attitudes and, simultaneously, fear and hope for his safety.

Phlonykus turned to White. "At your convenience, Doktor."

White's florid color was back, contrasting with the pale fur encircling his face. He manipulated the Gate control awkwardly in his gloved hand.

"Stand by, please—"

The red sun vanished.

Standing on the stainless steel plate, Tom recognized the familiar lights of the Gate chamber. The chamber was empty, the red door down the tunnel closed. Where were Stein and Walker? Perhaps they had grown weary of monitoring the empty chamber, gone off to rest.

White busied himself with the new spatial and temporal coordinates he and Phlonykus had worked out. Finally, White called ready.

They took their places on the platform beneath the gold floodlights. Mari glanced at Tom. Her eyes showed an emotion he had never seen there before.

Fear.

Had Doktor Phlonykus not been standing between them, Tom would have followed his impulse and grasped her mittened hand.

Reading the wall controls, White announced, "Five seconds."

They were thrust through the cool, tingling darkness into blinding light.

"Shields on!"

Phlonykus cracked out the command before Tom's eyes adjusted to the dazzling sunshine. He stabbed his glove under his coat and depressed the top of the rocker panel. Details of the surroundings blurred.

He was alone. The others had vanished.

"Dr. White? Mari?"

"Here, Thomas."

Mari's voice. Someone bumped his side. A gloved hand closed on his.

Except for that slight blurring at the fringes of vision, he saw his own body clearly. On the right, he heard the Chairman say, "Hold hands so we stay together. May I have a time reading, please?"

White's voice. "Accounting for time zone differences, shortly past ten."

"Less than two hours. The entrance to the facility should be in sight—" A pause. "Yes! There, on the slope."

Mari said, "That's at least two kilometers away!"

"Sorry we couldn't come closer," White said. "I wanted to allow a safety margin."

Phlonykus spoke with urgency now. "It will require at least an hour to reach the entrance. Then we must wait for an opportune moment to get inside. If none presents itself—"

Tom, responding to a tug on each glove, started to walk across the rocky ground crusted with hoarfrost.

"—we shall have to burn through the outer doors using Dr. White's laser. I hope that is not necessary. It will make penetration of the underground more difficult."

Impossible, Tom thought. But he didn't say it.

The air was thin, piercingly cold. He noticed a plume of vapor on his right. Another came from his own lips as he exhaled.

"Doktor, when we breathe out, the shields don't hide it!"

Mari found a partial solution to the difficulty. Fastening her coat collar across her mouth helped to diffuse the plume that seemed to appear from nowhere. They began trudging again.

Ahead, an immense concrete door was set into the mountain's face. Several small figures clustered around it. Guards, undoubtedly.

Shortly the intruders mastered the knack of moving together while holding hands. They walked faster.

In one way, this desolate plateau ringed by snowy peaks was less unnerving than Pompeii or the fortieth century.

There was no evidence that this was the year 2080, except for several curiously fluted masts poking from the mountainside and a large truck of unfamiliar design parked on a road directly below the concrete door. With its open rear bed, the vehicle resembled a futuristic troop transport.

Still, this *was* Mongolia—the heartland of the Asiatic power bloc. A country in which a white face would be instantly suspect.

The wind-scoured peaks thrust up all around, snowy summits lost in patches of cloud. The only break in the mountains ringing the plateau was a pass far to their left. The rutted road disappeared up there.

Tom shivered, not entirely because of the cold. His mind kept sounding a single word. Doomsday. Once the hands of the clock reached noon, *doomsday*—

While they were still a good half kilometer from the parked truck, the great concrete door slid back. Three Orientals wearing drab uniforms and carrying sidearms strode out of the mountain.

"Missed our chance," White whispered with a telltale leak of breath from under his collar.

The soldiers moved down the slope to the truck. Two climbed into the cab. The third swung a leg over and climbed into the open bed.

At White's urging, they quickened their pace. It was already ten past eleven—less than an hour till the computer automatically launched the orbiting radiation bombs. They formed a single file, accustomed to maneuvering invisibly now. At least Tom certainly hoped they were invisible.

They neared the large truck. The man sitting in the rear smoked a small cigar and anxiously studied the cold, sunlit sky.

Behind Mari, Tom moved carefully around the rear of the truck and across the road of frozen mud. Without warning, Phlonykus stopped. Tom collided with the girl, couldn't stifle an exclamation of surprise.

The Oriental stood up. Frowning, he scrutinized the area from which the sound had come. Tom ached from standing still. Surely the man could see him. *He was staring right at him!*

Frown deepening, the Oriental knocked on the rear of the cab. He jabbered loudly, pointed, then climbed down from the truck bed to investigate.

A gloved hand tugged Tom's, an urgent signal to move.

The suspicious soldier started walking in their direction. Tom bumped into Mari again, backed away as someone's foot—White's?—struck a loose rock, making it roll.

The Oriental wheeled around toward the sound, glanced down—

A grinding rumble up the slope diverted his attention. The great concrete door was rolling aside.

More soldiers began straggling out in twos and threes. They chattered among themselves as they headed for the transport vehicle.

Noting their casual pace, the man who had almost discovered the four began to shout and wave. He pointed to a curiously shaped watch on his wrist, then at the sky. The other soldiers understood. Moving faster, they piled into the back of the vehicle.

Someone turned on the engine. The truck lifted from the ground, riding on jets of air. The noise hid the sound of Tom and his companions running forward.

Tom dodged in and out among the soldiers still straggling out of the mountain. Brushing against one, he jumped back. The man whirled and registered alarm when he saw that no one was within four feet of him.

By that time, Tom had slipped by the guards with their oddly designed rifles. He slid his back against the concrete retaining wall on the near side of the door and darted in just as the door mechanism began to rumble again.

The cement floor vibrated as the door closed, darkening a long, dim tunnel. Had the others gotten inside? Tom groped for them, not daring to speak—

With a ponderous *chunk*, the concrete door shut. Startled, Tom saw Phlonykus, Mari, and White.

"What's wrong with the shields?" he whispered.

Frantically, Phlonykus fumbled under his outercoat, then ran his hand over the rough tunnel wall. "It must be all this rock. Somehow it nullifies—"

"Let's move," White interrupted. "We have thirty-four minutes."

Mari pointed down the tunnel. "There are the lifting tubes. We descend to the fourth level."

They ran that way, beneath ceiling hemispheres that cast a feeble light. The lifting tubes resembled two elevator shafts without cages or doors. In front of the tubes, the corridor formed a T. There, someone cried out.

Tom whipped his head to the left. An armed guard leaped up from a stool.

White and Phlonykus charged him, struck him with their fists, drove him to his knees. They tore the rifle from his hands and punched him twice more.

But the wiry guard had surprising strength. He rolled away, lurched to his feet, stabbed his hand toward the wall—

Panting, White leaped in to deliver a punch. The guard doubled. But his fingers had already closed on a T-shaped switch. As the guard collapsed, the weight of his body dragged his hand down, and the T-bar with it.

Instantly, sirens howled.

15

THE DOOMSDAY CLOCK

EAR-PIERCING, the shrieks multiplied. White snapped the T-switch to its original position. The sirens kept screaming.

"The lifting tubes!" Phlonykus cried, pulling out the nerve trigger that technician Lexx had provided. It was a long, thick wand whose muzzle end widened into a bell. A thick cylinder surrounded the wand at its midpoint.

Phlonykus stared at the Oriental characters above each tube. "This one's down," he said, stepping over the threshold. Unsupported by any kind of platform, he began to sink slowly.

Mari jumped in next, followed by Tom and White.

Descent was smooth. As the main floor rose past Tom's eyes, he saw soldiers racing from the far end of the tunnel to answer the alarms.

They floated down past a door opening onto a steel-lined corridor. "Level two," White said.

Suddenly there was a commotion below, a shout from Phlonykus. Between the tips of his boots, Tom saw the Chairman point the nerve trigger at something outside the shaft. He heard two corklike pops.

The third-level opening came into view. Two Orientals lay asleep, their weapons fallen nearby.

White drew his own nerve trigger, and none too soon. A fat yellow head popped into sight below, its owner registering alarm as he saw Phlonykus floating down. White aimed along the shaft's side, pressed the nerve trigger's firing stud.

The Oriental's eyes glazed. He pitched lazily into the tube—a military officer, judging from his medals. The man turned slowly as the shaft pulled him downward.

Tom could hear jabbering from level four. Jackknifing his body forward through the door, Phlonykus disappeared suddenly.

Soldiers leaped into the tube at the second level. One jockeyed his curiously shaped rifle into position, fired downward—

Tom shoved White, then kicked against the tube wall to propel himself out through the door an instant before a bolt of white light sizzled down the tube. It missed Tom and struck the unconscious officer floating below. The officer disintegrated, pieces of him flying outward to splat against the shaft wall.

Tom shot out of the tube three feet above a parquet floor. The shaft's field let go. He dropped in a heap. White fired the nerve trigger—*pop! pop!*—at two men whose striped robes resembled the diplomatic morning coats of their own era.

Suddenly silence spread around them. Panting, Tom climbed to his feet. A fast count showed eight Orientals sleeping—three military men, five striped-robed civilians.

The room itself was immense and several storys high. Ahead, its semicircular wall blazed with lights and dials.

Among the lights was a row of clocks, showing the time at various points around the world. One clock, the largest, showed twenty-seven until noon.

In startling three-dimensional color, monitor screens displayed images of rocket launching pads. Each pad held a slender missile topped by a spherical pay load capsule. The radiation pods!

Mari stripped off her coat and gloves, ran past some benches set on a carpet in the center of the parquet. Uncovered, her hairless head gleamed. In her haste, the girl knocked over a taboret. An enameled bottle smashed. Clear fluid leaked across the floor. Rice wine? To celebrate the day of destruction?

The red minute hand of the largest clock jumped.

Twenty-six until noon.

"No one can enter except by these tubes," Phlonykus said to White. "Watch the up shaft. I'll take the other. If you exhaust your magazines, I have more—"

In the down tube, two soldiers floated into view, trying

to position their weapons for a shot. Phlonykus crouched, the nerve trigger angled upward, popping. The soldiers drifted downward, out of sight.

But more appeared from above. And others rose in the up shaft. White began firing. Soon the vast room reverberated with yells and popping, as though every bottle in a huge wine cellar was exploding its cork.

"Thomas—*help me!*"

In response to Mari's cry, he dashed around a large control console set out from the semicircular wall. More uniformed soldiers crowded both tubes. One managed a shot. White leaped aside. Where he had been standing, the parquet smoked, bubbled, then hardened into a three-foot depression. White fired again, again—

The clock hands moved. On tiptoe, Mari used a small power tool to loosen the bolts holding a section of wall plate.

Stretching, Tom caught the plate as it fell, threw it aside.

Mari pulled a probelike instrument from her belt. She inserted the probe among the exposed relays, turned it a half turn, then back a full turn.

"Now over here, Thomas."

Using the first tool, she uncovered a second bank of circuits, then a third. Tom caught the faceplates, hurling them to the floor.

Face stark with concentration, Mari bridged two connections with a tool that extruded a strip of silvery metal. One hundred and forty-four steps. She had done six—or was it seven? He didn't see how the girl could remember all the necesary steps, especially in their proper order.

The largest clock showed twenty-four minutes until the hour.

Mari's hands and forearms were buried inside a fourth opening. Suddenly smoke gushed from the interior of the wall. She leaped back as green sparks erupted like miniature fireworks.

"That is the last of the recircuiting," she breathed. "The rest is programming. It will go faster—"

She ran to the padded chair in front of the wide console, which was covered with switches and start-stops of different colors. Sitting, she wiped her palms against her cheeks, glanced once at the clock. Then she bowed her bald head, pressed a control with her right hand, waited, touched another with her left—

The lights on the wall began to change pattern, increasing speed in some places, going dark in others. Her hands began to fly, literally slapping the controls. On-off, *flash, flash*. On-off, *flash*—

By the tubes, the bedlam of shouts and popping continued. Abruptly, brilliant light filled the chamber. A familiar voice cried out. Tom whirled.

Mari screamed, nearly toppling from the chair.

Only Gordon White remained by the tubes. Doktor Phlonykus was gone.

And another bubbling depression was hardening in the floor.

White's nerve trigger popped, disposing of the soldier in the up tube who had apparently been responsible for the blast that had killed Phlonykus. The Oriental floated away, a smile on his sleeping face.

For a moment the great chamber was still. Mari's screams had dwindled to ragged sobs. Both tubes remained empty. Surely the enemy wouldn't give up—

"Phlonykus ran out of loads," White said, unscrewing the cylinder from the wand, then positioning a new one. "He was changing magazines when they shot—*Tom!*"

His shout spun Tom around as Mari ran past him, crying, "*Father!*"

Tom held her back.

"Let me go!"

"Stop, Mari!" He shook her. "Mari, there's nothing left!"

He hadn't meant to say it that bluntly. She started to go limp. Then she regained control. But she kept staring at the new pit in the parquet.

"Mari—look at the clock!"

He turned her toward the wall. Nine minutes till noon. The monitors showed smoke plumes rising from the launch pads.

"How many operations left, Mari?"

She touched her cheek. "Twenty. Twenty-one. I've forgotten—"

"You can't forget, Mari. Your father died so those rockets would never go up." He pushed her toward the console chair. "Don't make his death amount to nothing. *Mari, do you understand?*"

She nodded in a vague way. "My head hurts, Thomas. I can't seem to recall the sequence. It's all a confusion—"

"Try. You can do it." Lifting her bodily, he positioned her in the chair. "You're smart enough, Mari. That brain of yours—genius rated—"

White shouted a warning. A soldier in the down tube leveled his rifle. Tom dragged Mari to the floor.

A blaze of light melted the operator's chair. White fired back, missed.

Tom pushed himself up, and something made him say, "One of those shallow emotional reactions. I couldn't see you killed—"

White's nerve trigger popped again. A long sigh signaled the attacker's sleep. Mari stared at Tom with a curious expression as he helped her up. She laid her other hand on top of his. Then she hurried to the console.

The operator's chair had disappeared, its plastic fused into the floor like white swirls in a dark cake. But the console was undamaged. Mari began to hit the on-offs. Slowly at first, then faster. The clock showed seven minutes till noon.

White called Tom's name, fishing the Gate control unit from his coat. He tossed the control. Tom caught it.

"Hang on to that in case something happens to me. They seem to have given up trying to attack through the tubes. They'll probably try something else. They—"

He stopped, listening, as Tom pocketed the control.

"Hear that?" White whispered.

Tom nodded. "Like air leaking."

White sniffed. "There's no odor."

Tom located a source of the steadily increasing hiss. But no vapor issued from the ceiling ventilator. And he still detected no smell. Yet the evidence of his ears was unmistakable.

"Hurry up, Mari," White yelled. "They're pumping in some kind of gas."

Tom blinked, a ringing in his ears all at once. His stomach grew queasy. When he took a step, his legs were wobbly. Nerve gas!

Temporary or permanent?

No way to tell.

"Five more steps," Mari called, hitting another on-off.

The dizziness worsened. Tom swayed. The clock showed four minutes until the hour. On the monitors, smoke no longer gushed from the rockets. At three pads, technicians dashed back and forth, as if searching for the causes of a malfunction. With a little cry, Mari collapsed.

White grabbed for Tom's arm and missed, lurching like a man intoxicated. "Come on. I don't think they'll come after us in person now—" A racking cough. "Relying on the gas—"

The minute hand jumped to three before the hour.

Tom staggered after White, stomach burning, his head ringing, his fingertips numb. He had never been drunk on old-fashioned alcohol, but he imagined that this must be the sensation—an absolute loss of control of mind and muscles—

White knelt beside Mari. An image on one of the monitors was replaced by the face of a gaunt Oriental with many medals on his uniform. Behind him, other officers hovered. The gaunt man's eyes searched the chamber. Tom knew they were being watched until the gas took effect—

White cupped Mari's chin. "Did you finish?"

"One more—" She rolled her head out of his grasp. "One—"

Tom dropped to his knees, wondering if he could ever get up again. "Mari, this is Thomas. Stay awake. Is there one more step?"

Her flecked gray eyes closed. She held her stomach. "Dizzy. Sick. So sick—I—" She choked.

Tom knew how she felt. The nausea struck in swift waves. On the monitor, the gaunt man's lips peeled back in a smile. Silently, he spoke to those around him. Tom gasped, "One more step? What is it, Mari?"

"Can't—think. Sleepy—"

"Mari, what's the step? Tell me so I can do it."

"Can't—seem to remember—"

She was drifting deeper into unconsciousness. Like some surrealist vision, the clock stretched, looking almost liquid. Tom rubbed his eyes.

Two minutes before twelve.

Tom did the only thing he could think of—slapped Mari's cheek, hard.

Her head snapped over. She moaned.

Fighting his own lethargy, he helped White pull her to a sitting position.

"Mari," he pleaded, "tell me. Which control?"

The blow had revived her a little.

"The main on-off—"

"Which one?"

"Largest. Color code—purple—"

"How do I set it? Mari? *Tell me!*"

"To—on. Full on—" Her head lolled against White's shoulder.

Tom struggled to his feet. The parquet seemed to sway. When he looked down, it was *moving*—

The floor undulated like a black sea. The ripples worsened his nausea, brought a sour taste to his throat.

The central console seemed miles away. He lumbered toward it, saw the console melt, stretch, oddly elastic—

No, it's the gas. A trick in your mind—

Stumbling on, he wondered where he found the strength. Some will other than that of his dazed conscious mind—

One foot lifted.

Another.

Stumbling—staggering through heaving black oceans while the console seemed to retreat—

The clock jumped to sixty seconds before noon.

He reached for the edge of the console. His sense of distance was impaired. He missed, lurched forward, hit his head on the corner. With a cry, he fell.

The pain proved his salvation. It pierced his confusion just enough to let him grope upward, seize the console's edge, and hoist himself to a standing position.

As he gazed down, the switches melted together, gelatinous, unreal—

Thirty seconds remained on the clock.

Largest switch. Color code purple.

Why did the controls run like water? Where was it? *Where?*

Fifteen seconds. The sweep hand kept moving.

Hurry. *Hurry*—

Driven by a last-ditch strength he didn't understand, he found it, and then only because of its distinctive size and color. His hand missed it on the first pass.

Ten seconds, the sweep hand moving—

He tried again. Which way? On?

No, off.

No, on—

He couldn't remember. Nor could he comprehend the Oriental characters on the switch. Meaningless—

Five seconds.

Gambling, he hit the switch and rocked it to the opposite position.

Coughing, he started back across the black sea to White and Mari, mere specks, an infinity away—

Simultaneously, all the lights on the wall shut down.

Tom kept moving, driving himself. White's gesturing had the quality of slow motion. He wanted something. What?

The Gate control!

Tom fumbled it from his pocket and he reached the others. The great wall remained dark only a moment. Suddenly all the lights came on, along with a new panel not previously illuminated. The panel was a large red rectangle etched with oversize characters. It blinked on, off, on, off, like an alarm. On the monitor, the gaunt officer showed consternation, then rage.

"Control," White croaked. "Use—"

"We're—not in the open. The risk—"

"No choice. *Use it*."

But Tom couldn't. The box slipped from his fingers. Consciousness began to drain from his mind.

They would never get back. They would be executed for aborting the doomsday device—

What did it matter? He was sick, exhausted, wanting only to close his eyes.

He had a surreal glimpse of Gordon White's face as the scientist groped for the fallen control, lifted it—

Too late, Tom thought. Too—

Darkness.

16

3987—AGAIN

DISTANTLY, a voice. It seemed to be repeating familiar words.

Tom's sluggish mind struggled to make sense of them. He opened his eyes—

Remembered.

And recognized the man repeating his name. "Tom," Dr. Stein said, "where's Cal? What's happened?"

"I'm not sure."

Suddenly, vast relief. He was in the Gate chamber. On the far side of the platform, White groggily raised himself onto his hands and knees.

The aftereffects of the gas made it hard to concentrate. But the nausea and the ringing in his ears diminished moment by moment.

He stared at the other person just waking on the platform.

Mari.

She lay with her back to him, whimpering a little. His thoughts came in bursts:

Her father's gone.

Will she remember?

The gold floodlights make her hair shine—

Her *hair?*

Tom rolled her over as she came fully awake. He recognized her, yet he didn't.

Lurking somewhere behind the heart-shaped face of this girl with the long, gold-streaked auburn hair he saw the

141

old Mari—but only dimly. This girl's mouth was wider, her eyes more nearly the size to which he was accustomed. They were still gray, but lacking flecks. White noticed the difference too.

There was fear in the way Mari touched her hair. "What's become of me? Thomas—*who am I?*"

"Do you know your name?"

"My name is Mar—I'm not sure." The hope in her eyes faded, replaced by tears. "I remember my father."

With White's assistance, she got to her feet. The scientist said, "Evidently we succeeded beyond our expectations."

Desperately, Tom plumbed his own mind. Only fragmentary images existed to suggest what now lay ahead in the other—the new—3987. He glimpsed gleaming streams of blue water, a sky warming with stub-winged aircraft, a profusion of brilliant-colored fruits hanging in an orchard. The images made him think of his brother. "Cal's still up there, Dr. White."

"Or maybe he isn't. We'd better find out."

"I'd certainly be grateful for some kind of explanation," Dr. Stein said.

"Later," White said, hurrying to the wall.

Swiftly White reset the coordinates. All at once, Mari started trembling. "Don't take me there. I'm afraid of what I'll find. Of who I'll be—" There was terror in the new girl's voice all at once. "Perhaps I won't be anyone."

Soon White was ready. He stepped onto the platform. Tom gripped Mari's hand. She didn't protest.

The tingling darkness descended—

Tom heard a crack as the limb of the tree in which he had materialized gave way. He landed on his rump in thick, dark grass. Pear-shaped orange fruit rained down around him. The sun dazzled him with summery warmth. Nearby, at the edge of the orchard, Mari was getting to her feet.

Dr. White appeared. Without a word, the three walked toward the top of a nearby hill.

If this was A.D. 3987, they had indeed succeeded. The sky was clear, the air sparkling. The warm wind brought them scents of an abundant land. An animal resembling an albino chipmunk poked its head from a burrow, blinking at them as they passed.

"Seems obvious that the Asiatics never rebuilt the doomsday device," White commented. "Probably too costly and time-consuming. If I knew that Cal was safe, I'd award us medals."

Tom reached the hilltop first. Light struck his eyes— glittering light, from the mirrored faces of innumerable buildings. Low and geometrically shaped, the buildings began about five miles away, filling almost an entire quarter of the horizon.

"That is not my city," Mari said. "Oh, Thomas, that is another—"

She couldn't go on.

They heard a distant whine, saw some kind of train flashing along an elevated rail. The train disappeared behind a hill, racing toward the city.

"Obviously our best bet is to contact the authorities," White said.

"If they can understand us," said Tom.

"Let's see who we can find around that monorail."

They followed the elevated rail for nearly two miles. Then they sighted what seemed to be a passenger switch station, a large bubble suspended on gleaming rods beside the track. The bubble was reached by intricate metal stairs.

Near the station stood many vehicles. Peculiar, pyramidal vehicles, six-wheeled. A family was just parking one of the odd machines. Despite their curious robes, the man, the woman, and the two children looked reassuringly human.

The adults were only a bit taller than Tom and White, with normally contoured eyes, and full heads of hair. One of the children pointed at the trio.

Approaching the family, White smiled.

"Hello. Can you put us in touch with the police?"

Blank stares.

"Authorities?"

Alarmed, the woman jabbered in a strange tongue, then indicated the stairs. The family rushed off.

At the top of the stairs, the husband rapped on a window. A man poked his head out, looked, then ducked back inside.

"One way or another," White said uneasily, "I think we'll meet the authorities."

Shortly, a large, multicolored van arrived. It consisted

of two pyramids connected by a large cylinder. Rolling on twelve oversized tires, it stopped in the parking area. Three officers jumped out to question them, but the language barrier proved insoluble.

Tom, White, and Mari were pushed inside the vehicle's cylindrical section. The trip in the windowless transporter lasted half an hour. They emerged in a kind of garage and entered a corridor with walls and floor that glowed with shifting color patterns. Tom held Mari's hand tightly.

Finally, they faced an official with insignia on the shoulders of his robe.

The man was middle-aged, portly, and had a kind face. After several futile questions, he called for a rhomboidal apparatus on legs.

"I hoped Mari might know the language," White whispered.

Tom said nothing. The girl slumped on a stool, staring at her hands. Who was she in this clean new world in which humanity had not only survived but thrived? Probably, as she had feared, she didn't exist. His heart ached.

The rhomboidal affair proved to be a translator. From that point, matters were simpler.

The portly official was Echelon Chief Bomfils, the equivalent of a police precinct commander. The building was an outlying station. Trying to sound casual, White broached the subject of where they had come from.

Chief Bomfils grew agitated, sending aides scurrying. Soon, his superiors—an area commander and a zone leader—had joined the interrogation, which lasted three hours.

At the end, Tom knew they had reached the right year. Otherwise nothing was the same. Nothing.

Bomfils and his superiors had no knowledge of a doomsday device. In the history of *this* Earth, there never had been an Asian attack.

"An astonishing story," Bomfils said. "I regret to say that I do not believe it."

To judge from the other faces, none of them did.

Tom tried to think of proof. Finally he hit on a possibility. "Does time travel exist here?"

"Of course," said Bomfils, his voice filtering through the rhomboidal apparatus. "It is exclusively the province of temporal scholars in the learning hives."

"Who invented time travel?" Tom asked him.

"I am a defender of public order, young man, not a historian."

"Can't you look it up? Don't you have research materials available?"

The zone leader suggested, "A beam to the information vaults, perhaps?"

Reluctantly, Bomfils agreed.

Another hour passed. The Echelon Chief arranged for a light meal of bland, yeasty foods to be served to the trio. Then an officer arrived with a tiny capsule that was fed into a screen reader. Curiously shaped letters flashed by. Suddenly Bomfils pulled a lever. Unrecognizable characters were replaced by dimensional images. Tom jumped up. "That's my father!"

A moment later Bomfils focused on another image, and Tom got an eerie jolt. He recognized himself, although he was white-haired, and at least fifty years of age. He was posed rather stiffly in an office, next to a stooped, older man—

Cal!

Bomfils switched his gaze from Tom to the image and back again.

"There is a certain resemblance—" He paused, then addressed the other officials. "This is a monographic account of the twentieth-century discovery of the time-phase effect. There are images of the inventor, Linstrum, and his sons who carried on his work, Thomas and Calvin. Perhaps this one, who calls himself Thomas Linstrum, tells the truth."

Partially convinced, Bomfils ordered a city-wide search of police records. It turned up the presence of a peculiar patient in one of the larger hospitals. Via translation of his unfamiliar speech, the man insisted that he was a citizen of the past. Kept company by a metal box of unknown function, the man was recuperating from wounds.

"This report was circulated to all districts," Bomfils explained. "My aides did not bring it to my attention, since it had no application in this command."

"I'm sure it's my brother," Tom said.

"We will escort you to him."

Hardly hearing, Tom turned to Mari. His smile vanished when he saw her forlorn expression. He took her hand.

A police vehicle carried them into the city. With a population of forty-six million, Bomfils said, the city occupied the entire east coast of what had been, long ago, the United States.

The city was called Province East. Deep in its myriad of geometric buildings, so different from the towers of Doktor Phlonykus' doomed Earth, they reached the public hospital. It spread over fourteen blocks. In a huge ward reserved for indigents, they found Calvin Linstrum with Sidney Six hovering at his bedside like a mother tending a sick child.

The change in the future, Cal reported, had taken place without any warning. One minute, he was in his room in Phlonykus' city; the next, in the unfamiliar hospital. He knew then that the course of history had been altered.

"It wouldn't have been," White said, "except for Tom." He explained.

In Cal's eyes, Tom still saw rejection and anger. Something made Tom say, "I admit I forced the issue of going along. But I had to."

"I still find it hard to believe that you alone were responsible for aborting the doomsday device," Cal said.

Sidney Six quivered its stalks. "Dr. Linstrum, you are, on occasion, insufferable! Why do you bridle at giving your brother credit—"

"That's all right, Six," Tom interrupted. "I don't mind. From now on, I won't have to push so hard." He spoke the words with a cool, relaxed certainty that was altogether new.

"Push?" Cal repeated.

"To prove something."

"What?"

"I wasn't sure of myself, Cal. I wasn't sure whether you might not be right. I never admitted that till now, but it was there, pushing me. I feel badly about walking out on you in the other hospital. But it had to be done. Now that we're back—well, I know I'm as capable as the next person. I accomplished something I can be proud of." He looked straight at his brother. "And no one can take that away."

"I'll testify that he handled himself well," White said. "Mari and I certainly didn't have the power to make it to the doomsday console. But he did."

"I've been thinking about that too," Tom said. "Something gave me the strength—drove me. Probably you, Cal.

Ironic, huh? You were responsible for saving the human race after all."

"We can discuss psychological niceties another time," Cal snapped.

Initially disappointed by his brother's all too typical reaction, Tom soon realized that he couldn't expect Cal to change his behavior in a moment. Indeed, he would probably never change much at all. What had changed was Tom's own attitude. Even in these unfamiliar surroundings, he felt more relaxed. There was less need to retort, to argue, to *prove*. He had done the proving inside the mountain in Mongolia. And he had proved his competence to the most important person of all—himself.

In time, perhaps Cal would recognize him as an equal. The history that Bomfils had quoted offered hope.

"The sooner we return to where we belong, the better," Cal was saying. "The doctors keep telling me that I have to rest a few more days. But I'm perfectly well—"

He swung his thin legs off the bed. Suddenly his cheeks paled. He swayed and sat down.

A chubby head poked around the screen at the end of the bed. "If I may be so bold—"

An aide with one of the rhomboidal translators followed Echelon Chief Bomfils, who came right to the point. "What you have revealed to us this afternoon is both startling and significant. Therefore, before you return to— ah—your own time, we feel it would be valuable for us to have your transcript of the highlights of this remarkable affair."

Automatically, every head turned toward Cal. Even Six's stalks pointed that way. Tom didn't feel angry. He accepted the fact that Cal would be the voice of their father until Tom gained his confidence. He made a mental note to speak to Bomfils in private.

In a moment, Cal handed down his answer. "All right, a transcript. But fast. I want to go through the Gate as soon as possible."

Bomfils nodded to agree.

A police vehicle bore them out to the orchard the following evening. On the way, Tom said to Cal, "On the subject of my studying marine biology—"

"We'll discuss that another time."

"That's the point. There's nothing to discuss."

"What do you mean?"

"Marine biology's out. According to the monograph on the early years of the time-phase effect—"

"When did you read that?"

"Last night. Bomfils made it available."

"I wondered where you went for five hours."

"It's fascinating stuff, Cal. It says we worked together in the department. The Gate was my career as well as yours."

"I'm not sure you're really qualified—"

"History says I am," Tom grinned. "Or *was?*" He patted his pocket. "Bomfils provided a hard copy, translated into what he calls Old English. Our English. You can read it sometime. But the monograph definitely says we were co-directors of the department."

Cal went, "*Hmmph.*"

"A remarkable document," buzzed Sidney Six, hemispheres flashing. "I perused it over your brother's shoulder. Indeed, I can hardly wait to write my book."

"Your what?"

"My narrative of this adventure! The first published account of the operation of Department 239-T! Not a mere gaggle of press dispatches, mind you. A best-selling book!"

"I'm afraid there already is," White told him. "I looked at the monograph too. Six published his book in the autumn 1988. Archibald wanted to close the department, but as soon as the book appeared, he couldn't."

"Historically speaking—ahem—the die is cast. But don't fret, Dr. Linstrum. I will gloss over your personality defects."

Cal fumed as Six continued. "Now please pardon me while I file away a few more impressions before we depart. For my last chapter, you know."

Flashing its hemispheres twice, the machine began to mutter to itself.

Cal glowered. Tom concealed his amusement.

A moment later, Mari broke the silence. "I am still not certain that I should go with you."

Grumpily, Cal said, "That's all settled. There's no life for you here."

"But I feel so strange, Dr. Linstrum. No longer the same as I was—" The girl touched her long hair.

"No longer genius rated?" Tom smiled, gratified when

she smiled back. He took her hand. "That doesn't bother me a bit."

To his brother he said, "Do you really know why she decided to come with us?"

"I persuaded her that it was the only sensible course."

"And I showed her the monograph. I not only worked with you at the Gate, Cal, I raised a family. You never married, by the way. Too busy—"

Once more Cal looked ruffled. Tom went on. "The monograph includes several long footnotes on our personal lives. And photos of my two sons. One of them took over operation of the Gate after we died."

Cal started. "You know how long we lived?"

Tom patted his pocket. "It's in here."

"When— That is, when did I—"

"I'm not going to tell you. It's the one section of the monograph I'm sorry I read. And I'm going to tear it out before I let you see it."

"I insist that you—"

"No."

Cal started to speak again. He stared at his younger brother, and didn't.

"Anyway," Tom said, "The footnote of real interest was the one about my wife. She was a girl who found out that the heart is a little more than a circulatory organ after all. Her name was Mari."

She smiled at him then, warmly, completely.

The vehicle glided to a halt. Echelon Chief Bomfils appeared outside the hatch. "We have arrived."

In the balmy dusk, they walked up the hill into the orchard. The geometric city glowed along the northern horizon. Sweet aromas drifted from the trees.

"Where's the control?" Cal asked.

With a wry expression, Gordon White surrendered it.

"Some things never change, do they?" White murmured. Tom smiled.

Calvin Linstrum was too preoccupied to notice.

About the Author

John Jakes was born in Chicago. He is a graduate of DePauw University and took his M.A. in literature at Ohio State. He sold his first short story during his second year of college, and his first book twelve months later. Since then, he has published more than 200 short stories and over 50 books—suspense, nonfiction, science fiction, and historical novels. His novels comprising the American Bicentennial Series were all bestsellers, and his books have appeared in translation from Europe to Japan. Originally intending to become an actor, Mr. Jakes has manifested a continuing interest in the theater by writing four plays and the books and lyrics for five musicals, all of which are currently in print and being performed by stock and amateur groups around the United States. The author is married, the father of four children, and lists among his organizations the Authors Guild, the Dramatists Guild, and Science Fiction Writers of America. In 1976 he was awarded an honorary doctorate by Wright State University for his contribution to the nation's Bicentennial observance.